DEEP OCEAN
WOMAN IN'NA WATER

STEFANEI FREEMAN

Deep Ocean / Stefanei Freeman — 1st ed.

Paperback ISBN 979-8-9865979-0-4

Hardcover ISBN 979-8-9865979-1-1

FOREWORD

Over the course of my life, this work of fantasy has been many things for me. Since inspiration first struck me in the late 90s, to the recent years that have been transformed by one once-in-a-lifetime event after the next. Whether it's been a daydream or a security blanket, it's also always been a story. A story I am sharing with the world in hopes that the mermaids here—ones that look like me and my aunties, my mother—have the power and the dignity that I'd love to see more of in everyday life. Perhaps they look like you, too. Whether you identify directly or not, my hope is that their imagery leaps out of the book and into your imagination. More than laughter or dread or a potential cliffhanger or two, I hope this book broadens the horizons in your mind and in your life outside of these pages. Thanks to everyone who helped me believe that this could happen for me. I love all of you more than life, and I hope you never worry that I'll stop. Especially my mother and my dear husband.

PROLOGUE

It All Began With Happily Ever After

People once saw mermaids, come to destroy and come to save.
Evil men lost their fortunes and their ships to watery graves.
Compassion led the pod to swim slaves back to their beds,
Greed led the slavers to pay bounties on mermaids' heads.

A man once saw a mermaid, a couple lifetimes since those days.
He'd watch her visit sea caves until the tide chased him away.
Though her scales glimmered gold and dazzling light gave chase,
What he remembered most was the look across her face.

A mermaid once saw a man, though that's dangerous these days.
She'd feel him watching her while her thoughts were like a maze.
Though she was too busy, too burdened to wait,
She one day called him over, feeling the stirrings of fate.

With time they were friends, then lovers and then one more.
With tears in her eyes, the mermaid watched her daughter run ashore.
She waits in that same cave, head bowed in a silent plea,
For her long-lost daughter to be welcomed in the deep, open sea.

The gulls called overhead. They circled as they investigated the area for the stray pieces of food usually left behind by a gathering of humans. The sun was higher than the birds, but the sky had just enough fluffy cloud cover and ocean mist to dull its sharp, stinging heat. Safe from the creeping tide was a wooden platform. And on that wooden platform were rows and rows of white chairs with scarves and flowers hanging down the back of them. There was a strip of white carpet down the center and an arch at the front, decorated with more of the same lilies and roses strewn across the backs of the chairs. Sitting in those chairs were people of all ages. Many of them shared similarities in their features on either side of the aisle. Casually dressed in similarly bright colors, they sat fidgeting and sweating, but, mostly, they were watching the figures standing under the arch.

A woman, standing on the left, was cloaked in a warm ivory dress. There were three others on that side in matching, yet variously cut, mint dresses. A man, standing on the right, was dressed similarly, but in a three-piece suit. There was a brace on his right knee that was showing through the ivory pant leg. Three other people stood on the stage in mint suits on the right side. The figure standing at the front was a balding man dressed in a crisp white leisure suit.

He adjusted the book in his hands and spoke. "Daniel, would you like to start with your vows?"

The bride turned her veiled head toward the gathered people watching.

"Hey, look at me, Zelma," Daniel said, as he held her hands in his.

"Yeah?" Zelma replied, brown eyes wide under the veil.

"Today is our happily ever after. It's just about you and me," he said around a smile that only grew when she nodded and squeezed his hands in return.

"Daniel, your vows?" interjected the officiator.

"I do—I mean, the vows, right!" He paused as a gentle laugh washed through the crowd.

"Most of the fairy tales we read growing up ended with the phrase 'happily ever after.' But today, I am marrying the love of my life and every day after this—whatever comes—I'll be starting my days happily ever after with a woman who has loved me without conditions and without judgment. I couldn't imagine in a million years marrying any other person but you, standing here before me, looking like a vision."

He took a moment to kiss the backs of her shaking hands before he continued. "You really are so lovely, Zelma Malone. I love all the creative ways you like to wear your hair. I love how your nose scrunches up when you laugh at me. The way your gorgeous brown eyes watch me is something I feel on my skin. I love those beautiful lips and how you use them to encourage me. I love your work ethic, and... that you supported me financially and emotionally as...As I transitioned my love for photography from a hobby, into a career after my a-accident." He paused, as his voice stretched and shook. With a deep breath he continued.

"You wipe my tears and listen to me when I get frustrated. I hate that my knee is busted, but meeting you during my physical therapy sessions was the best thing that has ever happened to me. Even when I'm in the wrong, you try to be so gentle with me. You are still there for me when I'm burned out, when I'm exhausted, when I feel so far from who and where I want to be. And I want to give you everything. All of my time, my money, my love. I want to help you grow into the woman you want to be most. I want to live happily ever after with you, every day, for the rest of our lives."

"And you, dear?"

"You always have to try to show me up, don't you?" she replied with a laugh, and he laughed with her. "That was too good, Daniel!"

She sighed before she started speaking again. "When you said the theme of our vows should be fairy tales, I thought you were corny. But, then, I thought about my life before you. I might've been fine a lot of those days. I had friends and family, after all. But my 'happily ever after' didn't start until you were assigned to me at the office that day. You smiled at me, and I might've loved you then, but I didn't know it. The more I let you into my life, the more joyful my days became. There was always a reason to laugh or to playfully fight you or kiss you. You believe in me more than I've ever had the courage to believe in myself." Her voice faltered, and tears began to fall as she gently pulled her hand from his in order to dab at her meticulously cat-lined eyes.

Daniel now used his free hand to wipe at his eyes, too. To the delight of their friends and family, Daniel lifted Zelma's veil carefully so that they could more easily wipe each other's tears. A moment later, Zelma took a breath and nodded to the officiator that she was ready to continue.

"You're the love of my life and everything I've given to you has come more naturally than breathing. When I fall, you're the first person to look back for me. When the future is bleak or uncertain, it's your heart, your smile, your unrelenting hope that inspires me to keep going—to believe in a 'happily ever after' with you. I love you so much, Daniel Cruz."

"I love you, too. So much."

"Lovely. Now, the rings?"

There was a significant pause. All the eyes as one locked on to one of the groomsmen, specifically the best man.

"Huh?" he said.

Daniel's eyes rolled back into his head and he took a deep breath before gesturing to the slightly younger man who was the spitting image of Daniel.

"Oh, yeah, uh—here, Kuya." He fumbled, getting the rings out of his suit pocket before handing them over.

"Thank you. Now, place the ring on her finger and say, 'with this ring, I thee wed' and she'll do the same."

"With this ring, I thee wed."

"With this ring, I thee wed."

"I now pronounce you husband and wife!" said the officiator with a warm smile.

Daniel's grin shook at the edges from adrenaline and Zelma tried not to bite her lip in anticipation.

"You may now kiss the bride."

Quickly scanning for the photographer, Daniel positioned himself at a slight angle to make it easier for his classmate to snap the shot. Zelma stepped a bit closer into his space and he met her, draping an arm around her waist. She lifted her hand to the side of his face and gently drew him toward her. He followed her lead until their heads tilted and their lips met. A delicate silence hung in the air before slowly the cheers rang up and broke the moment. They pulled back and shared a breath.

"And we'll live happily ever after." Daniel sighed into the hollow of her neck.

Zelma nodded and leaned in for another, quick kiss.

CHAPTER I
A STATUE'S MEMORIES

"So, you grew up playing around these caves?" Daniel said, slowly making his way across the sand on the beach.

"Yeah." Zelma nodded as she leaned under his shoulder and wrapped her arm around his waist so she could bear some of his weight across the uneven sand. "My dad and I would play here together when I was a kid. When he passed away, I went to live with my aunts in the city."

"And you haven't been here in years?" he questioned as he looked down at the zigzag parts at the crown of her head and beyond to the stretch of beach and cliff ahead of them.

"Don't look around like that! We aren't going to get lost. These caves aren't really large enough for it. The tide shouldn't even fill them all the way at its highest."

"I'm a little disappointed now, though. Wouldn't getting lost in sea caves make an exciting honeymoon story? I don't know how you talked me into leaving my camera gear at home..."

"You know how expensive that new camera was. And you know over-doing it now means we won't be going anywhere else the rest of the week. We'll come back later for pictures. Right now is for sightseeing, and there's something incredible in these caves that I want to show you. I'm sure she's still there."

The ground began to even out and show stone under the patchy layers of brown sand. She grabbed his hand and gently guided him along. Her giggles echoed off the craggy open cave structure over their heads. Occasionally, they'd stop for Zelma to shake the sand and plastic pellets out of her sandals or for Daniel to rest as they went.

They came up to an area of the caves that seemed to go deeper into the cliffside.

The ceiling of the cave had eroded enough to let in a large beam of sunshine. There was a figure situated deeper within the cave, and even with the sun shining down on it, like a spotlight, it was hard to make out exactly what it was.

"Ooh, is this what you wanted to show me?" Daniel asked.

"Yes. There's a great back story here, too," Zelma said, brushing a few stray braids from her bob out of her face.

"Okay, so what's the story?"

"Let's walk and talk. I want to get a closer look."

They headed toward the beam of light, and, as they approached the statue, they noticed a layer of carved, grey stone buried under the sand. It led in a straight line to where the statue was resting, partially submerged in a shallow pool of dark water.

"Well, here she is," Zelma sighed, as she paused in front of the statue. Carved in dark stone was a life-sized figure of a mermaid sitting on her curled-up tail with her hands resting in her lap and head bowed, as if in thought. Atop her head, her hair was coiled up in a complicated, braided updo accentuated with a crown made of rounded points, which peaked in the middle.

"There's a nursery rhyme we all learned about her as kids. It's been here like, my whole life, and no one knows who built it or how it got here. That's why it's as weathered as it is—but it's still so beautiful."

"It is incredible. I don't know why this isn't in the brochure."

"Maybe if the city hired a better photographer, they'd have better pictures for the brochure. I mean, maybe we should see if they're interested?"

"Yeah, maybe we should," Daniel replied, his eyes soft.

Zelma smiled up into Daniel's face before turning her attention to the statue once more.

"You know, there's tales of mermaids inhabiting the water near our city since before it was founded."

"Really?"

"Yeah. Someone must've been touched by her story, so they had this statue commissioned or something."

"She looks sad. There isn't all that much detail in her face, but I get that feeling looking at her. The stonework on the scales is impressive, too. Hey, Zelma, how did that nursery rhyme go?"

"Sure..." Zelma opened her mouth to reply but Daniel interrupted.

"You don't think I could get you to sing it, do you?" he asked with a flirtatious smirk.

"Maybe I'll teach it to you later because I've conveniently forgotten how it goes," Zelma replied without looking at him.

"Sure..." he muttered under his breath, prompting her to roll her eyes before continuing.

"Let's keep this moving so we can go get room service for lunch, okay? The nursery rhyme was about a mermaid who was thinking out here in these caves—about what no one is sure. A man stumbled upon her here, and they fell in love and had a child who grew legs. At some point, the mermaid was separated from her family, and this statue is an homage to her. It's here for people to pay their respects, as she waits for her land-lost daughter to return to the sea."

"Land-lost? I see what you did there," Daniel interjected.

"Puns? Me? No, it's actually in the rhyme," Zelma said with a toothy, sunny smile.

"Gosh, you're so cute. I hope they get to be reunited somehow. People who love each other should get a happily ever after like we're having," Daniel said with his heart in his eyes.

"If only the world was like it should be," Zelma replied with a hand on his arm. "Apparently, we aren't the only ones coming out here because it's very clean. Look, there isn't even any litter. It makes me happy to think that someone's watching out for her."

"Hmm, and I get to watch out for you now, wife. Come over here."

She wandered closer. Daniel draped his hands around Zelma's hips, right where they rounded out into the tops of her thighs.

"I can't believe you put on that neon fanny pack with this beautiful sundress that fits you so, so perfectly."

"Fanny packs are perfectly functional! I've got spare water, sunscreen, my wallet and keys, my beeper, lip balm for when you get chapped because you pout so much..."

"Well, the eighties called, and they want their fanny pack back!" Daniel replied.

"That joke is so old!"

"Okay! Okay! But if the fanny pack is already back there, where am I going to keep my hands?"

"You can keep your hands to yourself when we're exploring caves open to the public," she replied. Daniel pouted and tightened his grip on her hips in response. Zelma giggled and placed a kiss on his cheek.

"And look at everything you have going on there!" Zelma exclaimed while gesturing toward Daniel's upper body. "You're making fun of me?"

She leaned in to nuzzle her face against the hair on his tan chest where his shirt was unbuttoned halfway down to his navel.

"You seem to be enjoying it."

"I'm enjoying my husband. You've got on a baby blue linen leisure suit, dear. Aren't leisure suits what old men wear?"

"Maybe—but they don't look as good as I do in this one."

She pressed a kiss into the tan skin against her face before murmuring in agreement. Straightening up, she turned her attention toward the statue.

"Before we leave, I want to say goodbye to her."

"I want to watch you from here—is that alright? I can't wait to come back with my camera. This would be a perfect shot."

"But you'd have to be in it, too?"

"Definitely for some Polaroids, but I'm thinking someone more beautiful is warranted for how scenic it is here."

He held his fingers together in the shape of a rectangle, framing her as she approached the statue. Suddenly, a shimmer of light caught Daniel's eye—as if something was stirring under the water behind the statue.

"H-hey, Zelma, come back over here."

She shooed Daniel away as she got close enough to reach out and place her hand on top of the mermaid's folded ones.

"Zelma, I think there's something—"

Daniel's sentence was cut off because, before she could turn to face her husband, she found herself completely submerged in water. She was bewildered because the water shouldn't have been deeper than her ankles. She flailed wildly and grasped for something solid but only felt sand and something like wet hair slipping through her fingers. The water began to trouble itself, and the shock of that had her gasping.

She started to choke, as tears welled up behind her tightly closed eyelids.

"Dan...! Daniel!" Zelma screamed with a gasp, barely breaking the surface for a moment before the sensation of being pulled under stole her voice once more. Only this time the water was heating up. Between the roiling bubbles and the warmth, Zelma fleetingly recalled ducking under the jets in her aunt's hot tub when she was a child.

She began to thrash so hard that her legs were tingling, almost numb. She couldn't resist the urge to press her thighs together around the intensifying ache in her legs, but instead of giving up, she kicked her legs harder. The tips of her fingers and in-between became more and more sensitive and then, suddenly—along with her lungs, legs, and hands—her bones had become meltingly hot and malleable. Just as she began to think she would drown, she felt hands close around the sensitive curve of her left breast and under her right armpit. She flinched before realizing she was being lifted out of the water.

"Zelma. Zelma, please. Can you hear me?"

She nodded, unable to speak, and coughed up water when she tried. She realized she was laying on her back on the firm sand. She threw her arms out in an attempt to grab on to something solid and felt the familiar roughness of the Velcro around Daniel's leg brace. Finally, her body began to relax. She opened her eyes and gazed up into the brown, almond-shaped eyes of her love.

"Da-ahem, Daniel, what happened?"

Daniel's lips were moving, but there was no sound. His hair was wet and curling around the edges of his ears. The expression on his face was one she'd never seen before. His lush eyebrows were pinched in the middle. His lips, normally pink and smiling, were pointed down at the corners and his skin looked pale—as if his blood had stopped pumping.

Even through the worst of his physical therapy sessions, he'd never looked so serious. The backdrop of the cave opening gave Daniel a halo of sunlight shining in behind him. He looked to Zelma a guardian angel—who arrived too late.

Daniel's hands shook as he moved forward, and Zelma blearily watched him reaching for the buckle of her fanny pack to unclip it. She took a deep breath, thankful for the release in pressure, and as she tried to sit up, there was a great splash of water at her feet. She was startled and tried to pull herself away from the water's edge.

"Zel-Zelma, calm down."

She turned into his arms and tried to crawl up the sand, but the splashing only grew more chaotic behind her.

"Calm down? Daniel, there's something in the water! Don't you see it?" Zelma yelled with a fist full of his shirt in each hand.

"I do, Zelma. Look, please look..."

In some fit of delirium, she turned toward the statue for answers. Finding none, she looked down at her body to where her dress was still gently floating in the, once again, shallow water. Only, her sensible sandals had been replaced by a glimmering tail fin the color of deep black onyx. In a panic, she lifted her dress only to find that the scales crawled up her entire body. Her belly button was no longer there, and in its place were more scales that faded into patches on her skin.

Her hands had become webbed, yet her wedding ring remained snug. Her fingernails had grown pointed and black at the tips, like stiletto-tipped claws. She reached up to touch her braids and was relieved to find that they were still styled in the braided bob she had done before leaving for her wedding.

"Daniel, what happened to me?!" Zelma asked. Her voice shook with every word and her throat felt sore from coughing.

"I don't know, Zelly. I don't know, but we'll figure it out."

"Figure it out?! How?!"

"Wait, do you hear that?"

7

"No, I don't hear anything but..."

"Singing? Is someone coming?"

"It's so faint, but I hear it, too. Oh, no! Do we even want them to see us?"

Zelma and Daniel turned their eyes toward the statue and then the mouth of the cave. The humming grew louder. The voices, at least two, harmonized beautifully. A song that Zelma had never heard before, the voices were other worldly, melodic and...calming.

"I don't think they'd believe us...even if they see" he replied, yawning.

She turned her head back to the water, torn between nodding her head to the rhythm and yawning herself. "Are you getting tired, too?"

Daniel nodded and started to respond when he was interrupted by a splash. Where the water was once shallow, it was inexplicably deep again. Deep enough that the bodies of two people were submerged up to their noses.

The sun glinted off their scales where they broke the surface of the water. Zelma struggled to process the two figures floating at the base of the statue in front of her. More than their faces or the colors of their scales, her mind could only focus on one thing—what she was seeing shouldn't be possible.

"Hello?" Zelma called hesitantly.

In unison they began to break the surface of the water. She turned to see if Daniel could see them as clearly, but his head slumped over onto his shoulder. She splashed with her tail and nudged him with her elbow. When she got no response from him, Zelma shook with fear and helplessly watched the two shapes swim closer and closer to them.

The person closest to her had a head full of locs that were such a bright, orange red that they radiated color even soaking wet. Her eyes were like a kaleidoscope combination of shades of yellow and orange, and when the rest of her head broke the surface of the water, her lips were smiling gently.

"Don't be afraid. He's just asleep. It's a harmless song, I promise," she said. She spoke gently. The way the woman curved her words reminded Zelma of the English her father spoke over the code-switched version her aunts had taught her in the city.

"What?" Zelma replied.

The other person, one with close-cropped waves faded into their scalp on the sides, didn't come as close. Their eyes were almost pure white except for cracks of black around their pupils. They kept only their head out of the water and spoke next.

"We're like you, and we're here to take you home," they said. Zelma thought their accent was from some European country she couldn't place. It took a moment for the words to penetrate the fog Zelma felt in her mind.

"Home? You aren't taking me anywhere!" she replied. She turned in her husband's lap and reached up to lightly slap at his face. "Daniel, please! Please wake up!"

The others looked at one another and slowly came in closer as Zelma felt the strength leaving her body. Her struggles grew weaker and black began to creep around the edges of her vision.

"No—no, please. Daniel..."

She grabbed his wrist and held on. The last thought she could remember was that she never wanted to be away from his side and then she slipped out of consciousness.

～

"DANIEL!" she breathed but hesitated before opening her eyes. For a blissful moment, she felt the familiar weight of Daniel's body pressed against her from behind, lying as they often did when they napped on the couch. She thought of how she liked to use the softest spot of his stomach as a pillow.

Maybe everything was a dream, she thought to herself.

You must have vivid dreams...

Zelma jerked herself into a sitting position. She squinted at the dimming light of the sunrise. With shallow breaths, she looked around and realized she was no longer in the cave with the statue. She reached up to brush the sand off her cheek and realized, with a start, she was taking Daniel's hand with her. They were bound together with cuffs made of some shiny, black material. Daniel was still in a deep sleep, lying on a hill of wet sand.

Zelma's eyes surveyed the water that filled the cave around her. It was about the size of an average swimming pool with a small ledge of sand. She noticed flashes of orange under the surface and the water swayed gently from the shark-like circling of the woman in the water.

"Hello? You can probably hear me, right? W-what have you done to us? Where are we?"

The dark water parted around the orange locs of the woman from before. This time she was close enough for Zelma to notice the golden ornaments she had laced through her hair. The woman swam gracefully closer until she was just out of reach of the end of Zelma's tail fin.

"Take a look for yourself," she replied slowly, as if not to startle Zelma.

Though the light of the day was dying, Zelma looked around and could see she was sitting on a slab of smooth stone under a layer of sand. There was a small fire behind Daniel and a small A-frame structure built out of wood, trash, and palm fronds. There was no visible opening to the beach, yet there was an opening in the cave overhead.

"I-is this some secret place you take people after you...do whatever you do to them?" She gestured with her free hand toward the woman.

Zelma was completely caught off guard by the bright, cheery laughter she got in response to her accusation.

Upon closer inspection, the woman had what appeared to be plate armor across her chest and down to where her scales took over at her hips. Her arms were quite toned, and she was decorated with golden, glittery bangles, rings, and chains. She was gently treading water and used her hands to balance herself as she watched Zelma carefully. With ease, she changed her position so that she was casually floating atop the water on her stomach. Her tail, which was swirled with every shade of orange and yellow imaginable, swayed behind her.

"I've done nothing to you."

"How can you say that? Why did you drug or...lullaby us to sleep?"

"Okay, well, I did sing that song that lulled your lover to sleep, but—short of saving you after you transformed—I haven't done a thing to you! You passed out from the transformation. I promise."

"I transformed?"

Humming softly in agreement, the woman bathed in orange-gold cautiously reached out her hand. When Zelma didn't flinch away, she placed her hand on top of Zelma's inky black tail fin. "You are transformed."

Shrugging her hand off almost reluctantly, Zelma turned her attention to Daniel. "But when will he wake up?"

"It should be any time now. It was a pain moving both of you, but you really gave us no choice, did you? That's incredible how quickly you were able to tap into your power."

"Power?" Zelma repeated inanely.

Speaking slowly, but not unkindly, she motioned toward the cuffs adorning Zelma's and Daniel's wrists. "You bound yourself to your lover before you lost consciousness. That you were still able to use your ability in that state is a good sign of how powerful you'll become."

"Am I cursed? Do people just spontaneously change at the fountain? How has no one ever heard of this? And how do I get him unchained? How do I get me unchained? How—"

That's too many questions. But that last one is on you.

"Who said that? I didn't see your lips move at all!" Zelma said as she threw wary glances all over the cave.

"White, come out of that water. You can call me Honey and them White until further notice," Honey said over her shoulder.

"Oh, okay," Zelma agreed, nonplussed.

Their head popped out of the water but only at eye level. The water dripped off their stark white hair, and Zelma's eyes followed the droplets over their deep brown skin and down the rounded bridge of their nose. Those eyes, milky white with the same black marbling as their tail, were even more otherworldly up close. And the fact that they didn't lift their head out of the water to breath underscored the impossibility of what Zelma's eyes were telling her she was seeing.

"S-so, you're White and she's Honey?"

White lifted themselves half out of the water to speak but paused. Zelma took a few seconds to see that they wore only a wreath of soft white coral that just covered their chest. They were otherwise uncovered from their sharp collar bones down their abs to the sharp V of their hips where their scales faded in. After an encouraging look from Honey on their left, they swam further up to rest their elbows next to Zelma on the flat smoothed stone next to her tail.

"Should be pretty self-explanatory, yeah," White replied.

"Can...can you read my thoughts?" Zelma asked, half afraid of the answer.

"In a way. But you'll get better at projecting the thoughts you want us to hear. And you hear the thoughts we project to you."

"Oh, okay. I don't fully get it but... Uhm, you guys said that I put the cuffs on him? If that's true, how would I get them off?"

"I think she is ready for the talk," Honey said, locking eyes with White.

"Well, when two humans feel a certain type of way, they—" White began with the most deadpan expression Zelma had ever seen anyone have.

"White, you remember what this was like for you, don't you? She's scared," Honey interrupted with a hint of a laugh. "We don't have time for you to be cutting up."

"You know I love it when you scold me, Honey," White replied with a half smirk.

"What they are trying to say is that we have a lot to teach you and not much time. You see, your home is down on the ocean floor. We are your guard and guides until we can get you to where it's safe from humans," Honey chimed in, her voice high and sweet.

"Safe from humans?" Zelma began.

"And before we teach you everything you want to know, we're going to need to be sure that human you have there isn't going to go out running his mouth about mermaids in the caves to every other human he finds," White interrupted.

"But—have there always been mermaids in the caves?"

"Used to be. Now we only come up for special occasions," Honey answered, floating on her back now.

"I'm a special occasion? I'm just a normal person."

"Do you look like a normal person?" White responded with a raised, white eyebrow.

"Well, not now, but I did. I just don't understand anything," Zelma said as she scrunched her eyebrows together in frustration.

13

"Ehy, we are here to help you. Even White," Honey said, playfully splashing them with the tip of her tail. "Humans would be even more dangerous if they remembered that we exist. The ancient magic we use will abandon us the moment a human believes and tells another human, who then also believes, that one of us, by both our given name and our new name, is a mermaid."

"Wait, so what happens then?"

"Tragedy," said White.

"When the power abandons you, it leaves you as you were before. That means if you had almost drowned when you were transformed, then you'll be half drowned the moment the magic disappears. If you are deep underwater, you'll likely perish without help. And if you lived long, you could age decades in seconds. It's never, ever good," finished Honey.

"Wait, transformed? Did you transform me?"

"Aht, aht!" Honey answered with a finger pointing toward Zelma. "We didn't do anything but find you and take you here."

"Well, we did sing your human to sleep, but he should be up soon, so..." White interjected with a shrug.

"And we didn't mean for you to be scared," Honey added.

"You didn't make me sleep at all?" Zelma asked with a cock of her head.

"No, that was your transformation. Our magic hardly works on one another—not without incredible will behind it."

"What should we do with the human? Free him?"

"Her lover, stop saying it that way. She wants to get the cuffs off her lover, not her human," Honey corrected White with a stern look. White sucked their front teeth loudly in response.

"You guys can separate us?"

14

"You want us to?" Honey asked softly.

"Has he ever hurt you?" White asked, with an expression that was impossible to read.

The air in the cave seemed to thin with the intensity of their gaze. Zelma felt a flash of goosebumps raise up all over her skin. She rubbed distractedly at her arms and replied carefully. "No, he'd never hurt me. What do I have to do to keep him with me?"

"Traditionally, he takes a vow, and if that vow were to be broken, he'd be met with a curse," White answered as the tension fell in the cave.

"A curse?" Zelma parroted.

"One of your own design."

"And then you'll trust him, if he takes a vow?" Zelma asked.

"More or less. But we'd also need a way for him to travel with you safely. The depths we must live at are far greater than would be comfortable to any human. If we had the time, we could reach out to some others who could offer more options, but we may have to leave him here and come back later after we figure something out," Honey said while fiddling with some of the rings on her right hand.

"Hmm. Why not change him, too? Why is it just me?"

"Well, only the leader of our pod can turn people. Plus, our magic is soul magic. It only bonds itself to feminine souls," White answered and laid their head on the slab of stone and sand right next to Zelma on the other side of Daniel's leg.

"Wait, only women?" Zelma asked.

"Mostly? When I was found drifting out to sea, no one was sure I could be saved. Each year since my transformation has been the best year yet, and I'm not the only one," White replied as they swished their tail up and down in the water.

"I think you meant that you cause more chaos every year."

"Honey, we are creatures of passion—you can't blame me for that. And to your point, the chaos we create is used for good, so that makes everything good. Don't listen to her, yeah?"

"Humph," Honey replied.

"Anyway," White continued with a gentle roll of their eyes. "Does your lover largely identify with feminine energy? Do you think the soul magic would be compatible?"

"No, that wouldn't work for him. Uhm, about the curse, though?"

"Yeah, the bond we have with our magic gives us abilities far beyond any natural being. What we believe can be so. Your ability to breathe underwater and survive the deep pressures at the ocean floor exists when you will it to."

"So, I could be human again if I believe I am?" Zelma asked, hopefully.

"Maybe," White said with a smirk. "Try it."

Zelma scrunched up her face and remembered the feeling of walking down the aisle to marry Daniel just a day ago. After a few seconds of staring into the darkness behind her lids, Zelma snapped her eyes open to the sight of her tail gently moving with her breath and the waves.

"Not working?" White asked with a playful pout. "Maybe you need us to train you or...maybe your heart isn't in it to give all this up?"

"You are no longer a creature bound to the laws of nature but to the laws of will and magic, which is why you need to continue to desire to live. If you no longer want to exist, you'll pass on and another will be able to take on your title and power," Honey said as she swam up on the other side of Daniel's legs to rest her elbows and peer into Zelma's face.

"So," Zelma started and ran her hands through her braids as she thought. "So, we can do whatever we want?"

"Within limits, but yeah. Whatever you have the will for, you can do. Whatever skill you develop for channeling your magic, you can use. And whatever you have support for when you don't have enough will or magic ability, you can make happen with the pod. We find out new things every generation!" Honey said, and though her eyes were bright in color, her face brightened up even more from within as she spoke.

"She gets really excited about this stuff," White added.

"Does that mean you two have different abilities?" Zelma asked, looking left and right at the others lying on each side of her.

"We do," White said

"And they are...?" Zelma asked, holding out the last syllable.

"Are you asking for a demonstration?"

"Yes! Uhm...please?"

White straightened their back. With a deliberate air about their move-ments, they proceeded to shape their fingers into guns and point them in Zelma's direction before breaking into quiet laughter when Zelma flinched back slightly.

"White," Honey said, dragging out the syllable with a disapproving one.

"That was funny! I couldn't help it! We should give you an accurate demonstration—and we will. But first, let's talk about your plan for your lover before we get carried away. If your lover says no to the vow, we can alter his perception of today to keep ourselves safe—"

"I...I don't ever want him to be hurt. I don't want him to lack anything. I want him to be safe with me."

"I hope he is worthy of your devotion," White murmured as they laid their head back down into the cradle of their arms.

"You look like you have an idea?" Honey asked Zelma with a tilt of her head.

"I couldn't help but think of something like a message in a bottle," Zelma said. "Where there's a beach and he'd be safe and he'd live as long as I do. And if he's in anyone else's possession but mine, he sleeps like a toy or something so they don't know it's him and he won't be hurt if—if the bottle breaks," Zelma finished almost out of breath.

"Oh, to be young and in love," White said, and Zelma couldn't tell by their tone if they were being ironic or not. "I see why you married your lover—you must really want him with you. At least you aren't considering anything bland like making him bald—that would have to be vetoed. You'll have my support if you need additional magic, though I doubt you will in your case..."

"White!" Honey scolded and then blinked hard before she continued. "We'll need to come up with some clever wording to make all of that into a song."

Zelma furrowed her eyebrows and asked, "We have to sing everything?"

"Well, harmonizing makes it easy to focus energy and make our wishes tangible. Your power is always available, but it lies dormant until we bring that power into the world. That's the relationship we have with our magic. In return, it strengthens us, lengthens our lives, and gives us options."

"I think your lover is awakening."

Like they were magnetized, Zelma's eyes cut to Daniel's face. His brows were starting to twitch and his nose wrinkled a bit like a rabbit's.

"Daniel, are you alright?"

"A little bit longer, Zelly. Give me kisses..." he replied with a spacey grin playing at the corners of his lips.

"They can be a bit fuzzy when they wake up. Humans aren't used to magic, so..."

"Mmm, baby please..." he begged, his voice already deeper than the last time he spoke.

"Daniel!" Zelma squeaked in embarrassment.

With a snort Daniel, opened his eyes. Startled, he began to pull himself backward onto the sand with his elbows. Zelma rolled over onto her stomach and threw an arm around his waist to steady him. Placing her other hand on the side of his face, she carefully dusted away a few chunky grains of sand.

"Hello, handsome."

"Zelma? Where...where are we?"

"In a cave."

"I had this dream that we were...that you fell...wait. You still look different!"

Zelma nodded slowly, tearing up as she watched his eyes flash with clarity.

"That wasn't a dream? You...you're really a mermaid?" he said, his voice breaking halfway through.

"Yes, apparently I am," she agreed with a small, shaky nod.

"Let me see," he requested.

Zelma hesitated. Something in the little half smile hovering around the edge of his lips made her feel like he was more curious than afraid. She turned back to look at the two others but saw no sign of them. There wasn't even the slightest stirring of the dark water behind her.

She gestured to Daniel, mouthing the words 'two more' while holding up two fingers and pointing behind her. He nodded along but looked confused. Frowning, Zelma pointed to her tail and held up two fingers. Blinking, Daniel cocked his head to the side and Zelma sighed.

"Nevermind. Just—come here, Daniel."

She shifted so that she was lying on her back along the smoothed slab of cool rock and waited for him to approach her.

"Don't be scared. I'd never hurt you if I could help it."

"I know that. You're my wife."

He carefully got onto his knees. He hissed in pain and opted to sit on his hip and lean to the side instead. He didn't touch her right away but looked over her from the tip of her jet-black tail fin to the tightly layered scales moving up her body to where they thinned out above her belly. Cautiously, he pressed two fingers on the scales just about where her knees might've been in a mermaid costume and Zelma flinched.

"What did that feel like?"

"Like someone pressing down on your fingernails...but on my legs?"

"Wow. This is incredible. You—you never knew you could be like this? That mermaids exist?"

"No! Did you? Does anyone?"

"I don't know!" he exclaimed. When he went to touch her with his other hand, he pulled hers and the cuff along with it.

"What are these?" he asked, shaking the black handcuffs.

"Oh, apparently, I made them when we passed out—with my powers?"

"You have powers?" he said, gesturing wildly.

"Okay, stop jerking my hand around!"

"It's not every day you find out your wife is a magical mermaid, Zelma!"

"Is that still what I am?"

"What do you mean?"

"Do you really still want to be with me now that I'm like this?"

His face fell. "Oh, Zelma."

"None of this was part of our pre-marital classes, Daniel. What kind of life do you think we'll have together with me like this? Has none of this occurred to you yet?"

"Okay, okay. I'm not going to say 'calm down' because of what we learned in those classes—but why don't we start by helping you with that dress because it can't be comfortable being soggy like that."

"What? But what about what I said?"

"Please, let me help you, first?" he asked, bending his head down and slowly reaching for her. She sighed and leaned back on her elbows to make it easier on him.

He reached forward with his free hand and unbuttoned her soggy blue sundress. Leaning behind her with his free arm, he pulled at the straps around her shoulders, and she shuffled around to help him until the dress was almost free. With a regretful sigh, Daniel tugged hard on the thin spaghetti strap caught on the chain of the cuffs until it ripped in two. She was left in her black sports bra—saved from indecency—as she was covered in scales the rest of the way down. Without much of a care, he tossed it backward with a quick glance and realized there was a small shelter and fire on the barge of sand behind him.

"Well, that's convenient."

"Yeah. The others set that up for us."

"Oh, okay. One thing at a time. So, uh, why do you think I would take back the best day of my life? Because of this?" he said, motioning toward her tail, bringing her hand along with his.

"Okay, but you said your vows to a normal person, not..."

"You were never a normal person—and apparently you're the same as you've always been because we're arguing like always."

"Arguing? Who's arguing? I'm just trying to discuss the future. I'm not expecting you to what? Figure out whatever this is? Even if we wanted to leave, I can't walk and you can't carry me out of here. It wouldn't be fair not to give you an out."

"Okay, fine! You gave me the out and I don't want it. I'm in!"

"Daniel..." she replied with a slow shake of her head. "I can hear your brother calling you delusional for this."

"He's still single and he's an idiot."

"How can you be sure about this?"

"You're doing that thing where you're going to say I don't think things through, but I did think things through—when I married you yesterday. I'm not going to leave unless you want me to leave. Do you want me to go, Zelma?"

"No," she said. A single tear fell from her left eye and ran hot down her cheek. "I don't. I'm scared. I just don't know what any of this means."

"That doesn't mean it has to be all bad, then?"

"I guess not...but how are you taking this so well?"

"I mean, this is a lot. But I love you a lot more. I won't leave you. And I know you wouldn't leave me. Plus, can you imagine what I'd say to our families? That you returned to the sea like the mermaid in that nursery rhyme?"

"Or pay all the bills by yourself. That would suck. I don't know how you live in the moment like this, but today, I'm thankful for it."

"You're calling me simple-minded again, aren't you?" he replied. Daniel wiped a couple tears off his face with his free hand.

"Come here."

She pulled him toward her and nuzzled his face. Their tears and their breath mingled as the cave grew darker. Urgently, she gripped his handcuffed hand in hers tightly. She began to kiss his cheeks, neck, and ears as they cried and laughed and breathed the same breath for one long moment.

"Well, if you're going to be my lover..." she murmured in a singsong tone.

"What are you talking about?" he said with a laugh.

"Sorry, uhm, apparently, knowing about mermaids as a human is a significant thing. So, in order for me to be in good with the pod..."

"That's what you all call yourselves? The Pod? Sounds like a band name..."

"Focus. If I believe them, then the only way to be accepted by them is to take a vow, and if you break that vow, you'll be cursed."

"A curse...?"

"Yes. Well, only if you break the vow. Apparently, if humans find out that I am a mermaid and two humans believe it and—oh, I think they need to know my names. Apparently, I have a new one now; so, that's like two new names in as many days!"

"Who needs to focus now?"

"Okay," Zelma huffed in playful frustration. "If two humans find out that I'm a mermaid and they know both of my names, I'll lose my magical abilities. That could have dangerous consequences for me. Or maybe we could use it to turn me human again? I don't know. As for the vows, we'll have to sing some type of song where the lyrics will basically say something like, 'If you tell any living human that Zelma Cruz and whatever my mermaid name is is a mermaid, then some sort of consequence will befall you.'"

"Like what? Will I turn into a mermaid, too? A merman, I guess?"

"No. They mentioned something about the magic not working on people who have masculine energy. Apparently, the magic is alive? It has an aversion to masculinity and won't bond to it."

"I'm just going to pretend to understand most of this, if that's okay with you."

"As long as you are sure about wanting to stay. If this is all crazy, then singing a song shouldn't have any lasting consequences. And I can set up exactly what those consequences are so if you do break the curse, you shouldn't have anything we couldn't make work."

"So, no instant death? Or, like, my dick falling off? No, uhm, stumping my toe on the coffee table every day for eternity?"

"Yeah, and no pager batteries dying on you either."

"Oh, that's the worst. Such a pain to replace."

Zelma leaned in to run the tip of her nose down the bridge of his.

"I love you, Daniel Cruz."

"I love you, Zelma Cruz."

"Are you ready to meet them? I can't tell you how I know, but they're nearby," she said as she sat up.

"And here I thought I was nervous to meet your family the first time. Ow! You don't have to hit me, I'll be good!"

"Uh, come out?" she hesitantly called toward the empty, dark water in front of her as she massaged the spot she playfully whacked on Daniel's forearm.

"Maybe try splashing your tail around? Do they hear like sharks?"

"I don't know. I haven't been underwater yet."

"Oh, yeah, you haven't. Why don't we try it?"

Zelma held up their wrists. "I'm not drowning you just to try something."

"Oh well, about the cuffs. I mean, we could keep them. Like, after we're done with them today. We could keep them if you want..."

Zelma pursed her lips and shook her head side to side as she tried not to laugh.

"I can't stand you," she said, laughing anyway. They turned their heads toward the empty pool. "I wonder why they haven't come back yet. Oh, apparently there's also telepathy."

"I mean, I guess that makes as much sense as anything today has. So how do you use telepathy?"

"I think I just think really loud and want them to hear me?"

"Try it!"

Taking a deep breath, she gestured for Daniel to sit up and spread his legs enough for her to lean back into him.

"Oh, how's your knee? Being cold and damp probably isn't helping?"

"It hurts, but I can wait until we get the rest of this done."

"Hmmph."

"Zelma, I promise I won't push my leg too far, okay? I'll tell you if I think I'll injure it again."

"Okay, okay," she fussed. She took a deep breath. "I'm ready to try to get their attention."

With great concentration, she focused on the color white and on the smell of honey. She focused on how the two mermaids looked when she first saw them. *White, Honey, please come out.*

"Oh, uh, Zelma—uh, I think it worked."

Slowly two streaks of colors from two different tails began to creep toward them, growing brighter and more distinct until they broke the surface of the water with a small splash. The two figures, propelling themselves forwards using the webbing between their fingers, came to a stop before the intertwined couple.

Honey, looking at Zelma, smiled warmly. *You Called us. It was a bit clumsy, but we heard you.*

25

Hopefully you'll get better at Calling for help by the time you inevitably need us to rescue you, White projected toward Zelma. The voice in her head came with a sense of warmth that Zelma hadn't noticed from White before.

"Uhm, is anyone going to say anything or...?"

"Oh!" Zelma exclaimed and looked over her shoulder at her husband. "Daniel, this is Honey, and they go by White."

They both nodded but didn't speak.

"Uh, hi. I'm Daniel. It's nice to meet you..." he said, trailing off midsentence as they only nodded but showed no sign of responding verbally.

Oh, do mermaids not talk to humans? Zelma thought as she made eye contact with both others in turn.

It's tradition to avoid it as much as possible, Honey projected back.

But why? Zelma thought, curious.

To preserve our culture, thought Honey.

To keep us out of unnecessary trouble, White projected.

Zelma felt a pressure at her temples as she took in their thoughts simultaneously. She shook her head and continued to listen.

What we need to do is find a way to put your wishes into something you can harmonize, Honey thought with a serious expression.

"I've heard of speaking with your eyes, but this is—wow. You three are really understanding each other?" Daniel asked as he placed a hand over his knee brace and rubbed distractedly.

Zelma, equally distracted, patted his arm as she continued to make eye contact with the others as they treaded water in front of them.

So, what counts as magic? Do I just need to freestyle something?

Words help us understand your intentions so we can add our will to yours. It's tough to do on the spot, but we don't really have all the time in the world, White replied.

What if it's just bad?

We laugh and try again, Honey thought, smiling.

Okay. What about something like:

A message given, a message received.

If you break this curse, a message in a bottle you will be.

Zelma thought as she cringed and covered her face in embarrassment.

Our magic is kind, but you'll want to be more specific, Honey projected as she tried to peek around Zelma's hands into her eyes.

At least you're trying to rhyme, White thought and sighed audibly.

Okay, how about we make it longer? thought Zelma, before she lowered her hands and continued.

A message in a bottle you'll be, hidden safely in luxury.

The outside world, you'll hardly see, after speaking the secrets three:

Your wife's two names and...who she be?

You know, I give it a pass, thought White.

There was a pause before everyone, with the notable exception of Daniel, began to giggle. So, not to be left out, he began to laugh too, albeit confusedly.

"Daniel, why are you laughing?" Zelma turned and asked.

"The same reason...you guys were?" he said, his smile fading.

"Anyway," Zelma said aloud as she placed her hand over Daniel's on his leg brace. "I have the curse finished. Are we sure this will work?"

The two in the water nodded.

Zelma turned to gaze into his eyes. She could see him looking at the others, and she could make out the glinting of their scales in the dark of his brown eyes.

"Are you sure about this?"

"I'm just as sure as I was about my vows yesterday," he replied quietly in the calm of the cave.

"Daniel. I'll do anything I can to protect you. I don't want you to regret this."

"I couldn't. Did I ever think our future would lead to something like this? No! But I believe in you. I want to be here for this no matter what happens."

"Okay," she replied shakily. "So how do we do this?" Zelma asked, not looking away from Daniel.

First, you're going to want to remove the cuffs. This will be good practice for drawing out what we need for the curse, Honey thought.

Okay, so I just grab his arm. Zelma placed her free hand over his wrist where the cuff held firm and cool to the touch.

Now envision the cuff loosening. Hum if you need something to focus your power.

Gently, she began to hum a simple scale. First up and then back down, as she closed her eyes and stared into the darkness behind her lids. She brushed her fingers up and down the smooth material and tapped her black stiletto nails against it to hear the sound it made.

What type of stone is this? she thought. As she focused on what it could be, she felt the bizarre sensation of it melting in her hand.

"Woah!" Daniel shouted, and she felt him flinch his wrist from her grasp.

She threw open her eyes and looked down to see the stone melted like candlewax down their arms before evaporating into thin air.

"I...did it?" she said, bewildered.

"Yes! You did!" he replied, blinking rapidly.

Very well done. How did that feel? Honey projected, sounding proud. Zelma felt a curious echo of the feeling blossom in her chest with the thought.

"It didn't feel like much of anything, really. I was just thinking about it, and it happened. Like breathing."

"That's cool that it felt easy. Zelma, you're a magician now! I'm so proud of you!" Daniel said, laughing and rubbing at where the cuff once closed around his wrist.

"Thank you, everyone," she said with a laugh at Daniel's antics. "So, does that mean we do the vow and the curse?"

White and Honey nodded simultaneously.

Yes. May we touch you? White asked.

Oh, of course, Zelma replied.

Coming around to either side, they gracefully pulled themselves up into a sitting position on the flat shelf of rock that Zelma was sitting on. Daniel carefully backed up onto the sand and favored his busted knee as he went. Honey and White linked their arms over Zelma's shoulders and wrapped them around her rib cage on both sides. Breathing deeply, Zelma leaned into their embrace.

She realized she should've been getting cold, but only Daniel was showing signs of the chill in the air and the water. She belatedly picked up on the fact that he was beginning to shiver. *Time to end this quickly and get him settled in for the night.*

Yes, let's finish this quickly. Let's project the words you had earlier but hum a tune familiar to you, Honey suggested. *Oh, and have your lover place his hand on you—the curve of your spine is a good place to connect to your power.*

That sounds good, Honey. Do you two know how to sing the happy birthday song?

They still sing that up there, huh? Honey asked.

Not really, but I catch on quickly, White replied.

"Daniel, can you get your hand on my back from there?"

"Y-yeah. Sure," he said.

We'll back you up. You really need to believe that the curse is real for it to take effect. If we can't sense that it's safe for us to trust him, we won't. You'll be able to feel when he connects with your magic, Honey thought helpfully.

The more they believe in the curse helps, too. Their fear usually works to our advantage. This won't save you if he betrays you, but it will make it easier for the pod to seek justice on your behalf, thought White, and Zelma sensed an echo of bloodlust in the projection.

Blinking with wide eyes, Zelma nodded at White before looking over her shoulder once more at Daniel.

Ask him to vow not to tell your secret, thought Honey.

"Daniel, do you vow never to tell my secret in any way?"

"I do, Zelma Cruz."

Touched, Zelma smiled and began to hum while White and Honey hummed along. Their voices carried in the cave, and whether by talent or by magic, they harmonized effortlessly. Zelma sang the words aloud while the other projected their thoughts.

A message in a bottle you'll be,

Hidden safe in luxury.

The outside world, you'll hardly see,

after speaking the secrets three:

Your wife's two names and...who she be.

Zelma finished with a laugh, as she ended the last line to the tune of "and many more." White and Honey smiled at the sight of Zelma's joy.

"Uhm, was there supposed to be fireworks? Tingles? Anything? That was beautiful, by the way," Daniel said, rubbing gentle circles across Zelma's back.

"No, Daniel, something is different," Zelma replied as she leaned into his touch. *I felt warm, like I was in the sun.*

We felt it, too. He won't know until he breaks the curse, White thought back.

"Uhm, they said the magic only kicks in if you break the curse."

"Oh. So, if I believe the curse and break it and then believe I'm cursed for breaking it, that's, like, a self-fulfilling prophecy?"

"I mean... A self-fulfilling prophecy to an extent, but if the curse is real, then you're suffering the consequences of the actual curse?"

Anyway, isn't your human lover getting cold? We want to give you two time together to collect yourselves—but first there are a few things you should know, White projected to Zelma.

Now that he's taken the vow, it's time for you to learn more about who we are. I'll start. My name is Citrine. I'm not sure what you know about gemstones, but the coloring of my scales and eyes should've given me away, thought Honey-now-Citrine.

And I'm Howlite, which is why I'm so formidable, added White-turned-Howlite with a bow of their head.

And I'm some kind of stone? Like marble? Can't I just stay Zelma? Zelma asked.

They smiled in unison, showing all their teeth. *You're more than who you were on land. Taking on the name makes you one of us. You already have one. I'll give you a hint. It starts with an O,* Citrine thought helpfully.

It's the color all over your scales...

It's found near volcanoes...

Oh! I know this from that geology class I took forever ago! I'm Obsidian? My new name is Obsidian?

Yes. It's up to you if you'd like to tell your partner. But, seeing as there will be consequences and you trust him dearly...it should be alright.

Oh, no, Zelma thought suddenly with a frown.

Yes? Citrine replied.

"Zelma, are you alright?" Daniel asked.

What if the curse is broken in public? Zelma thought with uncertainty building in the pit of her stomach.

Humans are generally oblivious to magic. But should it happen on camera or in front of humans, there's typically a fuzziness around acts of our magic. It protects itself. Are you having second thoughts on his trustworthiness? Citrine projected.

No. I'm more worried for anyone discovering, well, mermaids. Us, I suppose.

Don't worry about that as much as training tomorrow, Howlite thought.

Training?

Yes. We're to prepare you to dive deep, so that you can return with us to the palace. There are so many waiting for you, Citrine thought with another smile that touched her eyes.

This is going to be the first Welcoming Ceremony in a half century, Howlite thought.

And we've got to find what type of magic use you have an affinity for. Though I think I already know what it is... Citrine thought with a sense of giddy excitement.

Oh, yeah, I thought that, too, Howlite added with a nod.

Affinity?

"Zelma? You seem better now?" Daniel asked again.

Because our magic infuses with our souls, there are infinite ways we can draw out our abilities. I have an affinity for stealth and transformative magic. Citrine has affinities for strength and healing, thought White.

You guys must make a good team.

We guard the sorceress because we're the best. That's why we're guarding you, too, Citrine projected with pride in her tone.

The sorceress?

She's the leader of our pod. There's really just so much to tell you— Citrine started before she was cut off.

"Zelma?" he said, loud enough to echo and startle himself in the cave.

Turning toward Daniel for the first time in what must've been minutes, she looked into his face and realized he'd been biting his lips to hide his shivering. His eyes were troubled and tired.

"I think that's enough for now," Zelma said aloud.

We'll be ready. Call to us as you did before. If you dig under the little shelter there, you'll find a chest that will make your lover more comfortable.

"Thank you," she called as she watched them swim away from the sand and straight down, their tails splashing a bit of water in parting.

"Daniel, I'm ready."

"W-why did you switch over to talking out loud?"

"I know you feel better when you can follow what's going on. I'm going to need you to dig a bit under the shelter. They said they left some things for us."

"Dig?" He pouted. "Can you believe our hotel suite is going to be empty tonight?"

"Daniel! Focus, please. I don't want you to get too cold."

"You aren't cold?"

"Not really, especially if I don't think about it."

"That's so amazing."

"Boy, go dig!"

"A mermaid is telling me to dig up a treasure chest. What a day..."

Turning around, Zelma watched him dig carefully with his hands as she shifted her weight onto her elbows. She used her tail to beach herself on the sand to better see what he was digging.

"What kind of treasure chest is this?" he said with a laugh as he pulled up a large orange cooler. He dusted the sand off the wheels at the bottom and tugged it toward the fire.

"Someone probably left it behind. It's kind of terrible, but the ocean is like a giant 'lost and found' at this point."

"Yeah. Woah, there's a change of clothes in here, some nuts, and a jumbo flask of water—I think. And wine or alcohol of some sort. It's like a corner store in here."

"Really?"

"Yeah, there's also some kind of oil, cheese, and canned sardines. And utensils? Some bottles with symbols on them. And a blanket folded into the bottom. Plus, you notice that this fire hasn't even needed a little bit of tending? Magic is like being rich!"

"You said there was clothing? It's got to be warmer than what you have on. Get changed. Now."

"Oh? Are you sure this is about my health, or are you just looking for an opportunity to watch me undress, wife?"

Holding her head up with her hands, she replied, grinning, "Two things can be true at the same time. Now, strip."

"Yes, ma'am."

They fell silent as she watched him untuck the front of the powder blue linen button up that was practically soaked through. As he shrugged the loose top off his shoulders and reached for his belt, Zelma tracked the caress of the shadows along the golden undertone of his tanned skin.

"Mmm, you are perfect, Daniel," she said as her voice dipped down an octave.

"Me?" he replied in kind as he slipped his belt out of the loops. He drew his linen trousers and white boxer briefs down in one smooth motion before he looked up. "Have you seen yourself?"

"Mmm, I'm too busy looking at you. Oh, take your brace off, too. It can't be comfortable with it being damp like that."

"It's never comfortable, but yeah. I'll throw the blanket down first so I can sit without sand getting...everywhere."

She laughed in response and bit her lip as he turned around to grab a pair of warm-looking sweatpants out of the cooler and carefully tugged them on.

"I guess I'm going commando. But these fit pretty good and they're really soft, so I guess it balances out. Oh, whoa!"

"What now?"

"Your lips. Your face changed earlier when you were doing magic, and it's changed again now."

"I'll let you tell me what I look like if you keep moving to get that sweater on and that blanket out."

"Yeah, let me just get it over my head... oh, whoa!"

"What?!"

"I-I'm clean. Like, when I put on the top and the bottoms together, I felt clean. I feel like I just showered and threw on lotion... What kind of... I'm even warm like I got out of a shower!"

"Oh. I mean, I don't know how clean you can get without a shower, but I'll take your word for it. You know, the dark teal sweater and grey sweats really suit you. Are you feeling more comfortable now?"

"Yeah. I just keep getting reminded that this is all impossible."

He eased himself down carefully and pulled up the slightly baggy sweats until his brace was exposed. She heard the familiar sound of Velcro and snaps pulling apart as he carefully undid the brace and set it aside. He left his leg extended as he dragged the cooler closer.

Zelma watched him rummage through and spread out everything edible, along with the utensils, on the blanket. He started setting up one of the small, opaque glass plates with snacks.

"Did you like anchovies, I forgot?"

"Oh, just make one for you. I'm not feeling hungry."

"Do you not need to eat anymore?"

"I probably do. I don't know. But I'm good for now. Please, you eat."

"This feels weird, but okay."

"You can tell me how I look now. Maybe it will distract you from being the only one eating."

"Oh, of course," he said as he paused to take a bite of nuts and fish. "Your lips turned darker around the edges, and there are lines around your eyes, like a cat eye, I think they call it. It's a little strange seeing you like this because you hardly wear makeup. Oh, but the makeup only showed up when you were doing mermaid things or checking me out," he finished with a wink.

"Don't you try to embarrass me! You're my husband! Of course, I was checking you out!"

"Why are you mad at me when you like me, like me? Stop trying to hit me—you'll get me all sandy! Anyway, it seems to already be fading. That's incredible."

"What else do I look like?"

"Well, your skin is still the same gorgeous brown. Your hair is the same, and it's holding up well. I like how the braids of your bob frame your face. God, your nose is so cute—I want to poke it."

"Not with anchovy hands, you don't!"

"Okay, okay. Sheesh. But I like your lips like always, and like I said, the black color is fading—so they're looking more like they normally do. You have a few scales dotting your temples now. Your ears look a bit pointed and black at the tips, kind of like your hands, but you can see your hands. They still look perfect with my ring on your finger," he said, lifting her left hand to his lips and kissing the back of it.

"Such a charmer. And you're surprised I fell in love with you?"

"I try not to think about it too much. You could've found someone less annoying, but I try to have my moments."

"Speaking of moments, something I thought of when you mentioned the hotel suite is the fact that we are expected back to our lives in about five days. I don't know what our families are going to think at that point—"

"They're going to think we disappeared out in the sea caves probably. I don't want it to come to that, so we'll see if we can get this somewhat resolved by then or at least find a way to buy us more time."

"I mean, maybe time travel is a thing underwater?"

"I don't think anything could surprise me anymore."

"They want to take me down to the ocean floor. Apparently, there's a palace there. They mentioned that there are some ways to take you with me... Would you still want to come?"

"Of course. First, I love you, and we went over all of that earlier. But also, do you honestly think I could just live my life knowing I could've gone to Atlantis and I just passed it up?"

"Yeah, I suppose that would keep you up at night. I feel like this is crazy to say, but I've never felt like this. I've never won anything or I don't know... Maybe I'm some kind of chosen one? I want to find out more. If you come with me, there's nothing else stopping me."

"That settles that. So, we're going to have to trust them? They haven't hurt us so far."

"That's true. I still don't understand how this happened. I hadn't seen that statue since I was a young kid, like six. I don't remember transforming then."

"Would you remember that? Also, something wasn't right earlier. There was a flash of gold in the corner of the cave and suddenly you were in the water, but I swear, I swear you didn't walk over there. You just glitched in and out of time. Maybe teleported? It's hard to say but..."

"I mean, that's how it felt for me, too, but it's honestly a bit hazy now."

"Yeah, I barely remember anything after that. I think there was singing."

"Yeah, the singing is apparently a curse to put humans to sleep. I'm not sure if it works the same on all humans or not. There's going to be some type of training tomorrow, so we'll see. They said something about affinities—like each of us has some way in which we're best at using our powers."

"Oh, like the handcuffs?"

"Maybe. Citrine—that's Honey's real name—has an affinity for healing. Oh, but she's also a fighter by trade, I guess? And Howlite, or White, is some kind of stealth expert, but they mentioned transformation magic, too, so...?"

"Wow. So, they use fake names in front of others to avoid the curse on you guys, right?"

"Yeah, so that no one finds out about them. They could technically be watching us and we'd have no idea because we don't know anything about mermaid magic."

"What? I just changed!" he said, covering his nipples despite having on a sweater with a look of mock horror.

"If it helps, I don't feel like they're nearby? I know you're joking, but I'd bet you're safe. We just don't have any choice but to trust them, as you said. Unless we find out how to use magic to help you carry me to shore and have me dissected by scientists at Area 51..."

"Never. Not ever. Not even for a joke," he said and lowered his hands to reach for Zelma's again.

"I'm pretty sure they focus on aliens and not mermaids, anyway. You done eating?"

"Let me get it put away," he said as he busied himself collecting the remains of his light meal to put back into the cooler.

"Good. After that, let's get you to sleep. Want to hold hands until the sun comes up, like always?"

"Mmmhm," he replied as he settled himself in for the night on his side facing Zelma where she was lying partially in the shallow water of the stone shelf. "Zel, can you say the poem again for me? Before I fall asleep?"

She turned her face toward him where he rested with his eyes already closed. *The last line should be enough, he's so tired.*

"A statue with eyes waiting to see, her long-lost daughter return to the deep, welcoming sea," she whispered to her husband, the cave, the waves, and the deep, dark sea below. "Here I come."

CHAPTER 2
WHAT LIES FORGOTTEN ON THE OCEAN FLOOR

ou must be so dry.

"Dry?" she repeated with a voice that was stiff and creaky from sleep. Blinking her eyes open, Zelma realized she'd managed to fall asleep on her back in the sand and that her fingers were numb and sweaty where they clasped Daniel's. "Ugh, what time is it?"

Daniel stirred in his sleep and rolled over to face the fire that had burned safely unattended throughout the night.

No need to wake him. Let's keep this between us. It's just after dawn.

I still can't get over how we can read each other's thoughts, Zelma projected.

She turned her head to watch Howlite floating easily on their back with lethargic undulations of their tail.

No. Normally, we project our thoughts to one another. You may not realize it, but you are thinking about me—willing me to understand you. If someone is reading all your thoughts, that's more developed magic...and not a great position for you to be in.

Okay. Hmm.

What?

Does this affect what language I think in?

You're one of those. I know a few people in the palace who are going to love you...

One of those what?

The type with a lot of questions.

Is that a bad thing?

I said there were people who would love you, didn't I?

Hmmm...

Howlite smirked at Zelma and used a hand to half-heartedly splash her. *As far as your questions about the languages, I wouldn't be surprised if our magic translates on our behalf. There are mermaids that have spoken every kind of language in the pod at some point, but when we speak like this, telepathically, we all understand the same.*

I guess I am "one of those" because everything you say is giving me more questions—not less.

C'mon. You'll need to keep this energy as we run through some basic techniques to get you ready to descend. You have no idea what you can do yet.

Is she still drying out on land?

With a jolt, Zelma realized she could hear Citrine project from somewhere deep in the water of the cave.

How'd you guess, Citrine? She's seconds away from shuffling over like a sleepy seal on her belly.

No matter how many years go by, the new mermaids always try to get around like that.

I'm right here, you two, thought Zelma with a flash of irritation.

We know you can hear us, Obsidian. That's why it's fun.

Citrine's muscular arms, layered with rings and bangles, broke the surface of the water as she emerged to her waist.

"Zelma? Where are you going?" Daniel called from the beach. He'd rolled over toward the water, but his eyes were still closed.

"Howlite and Citrine are here. We're not leaving the cave. You can just sleep a while longer. I think there's more food, if you're hungry."

"Mmmhmm, love you. Can I have a kiss?"

With a roll of her eyes, Zelma reversed course feeling inelegant as she shuffled over, employing a mix of a wiggle and a horizontal body-roll. Daniel took pity on her and crawled over to meet her halfway, their lips pressing together gently in the middle.

"Hmm, I am really dry. I hope my lips didn't bother you," she said, running her tongue over her lips and his incidentally.

"Of course not. It's crazy, you don't even have morning breath."

Oh, I found this for your lover. Tell him to catch it.

"Daniel, you should—" Before she could finish her sentence, a small toothbrush kit sailed from Howlite's fist as they hurled the object toward him and knocked him upside the head, tousling his messy bed head even more. "Catch that…"

"What is this? Ow, thank you!"

Throwing a nod toward Daniel, Howlite, without any sign of exertion, beached themselves on the sand next to Zelma. They then began to billow their tale toward the water, wiggling side to side, and—with just a few repetitions of these movements—Howlite was back in the water again.

"Oh, like that," Zelma said aloud.

Focusing, she began to wiggle her hips and fin in strategic movements, digging in with her elbows. She looked up to see Daniel watching her sleepily, curled up on his side and using his arm as pillow.

Much better than a seal, yeah? she thought, turning back toward Howlite.

Seals are more athletic when they aren't sleepy, and you're getting there.

Wait, I'm in backward—I mean, my tail is in the water, but how do I turn around?

Just come in all the way. Are you afraid you'll drown?

You know, your skin is crawling. You've been drying out with all that sand everywhere. I bet you'll feel it more if you think about it, Citrine projected unhelpfully.

I do now! Isn't that how our power works? So, shouldn't I not do that?

It was strange, but when one of the others laughed during one of their telepathic conversations, Zelma couldn't hear the sound of laughter. Instead, she'd get a hint of a warm feeling in her chest or a twitch around the corners of her mouth.

Pushing herself the rest of the way, she entered the dark, cool water with hardly a splash. She had closed her eyes on instinct but opened them consciously, and to her surprise, the salt didn't sting at all. As she swayed using her fin, she realized she couldn't feel the bottom of the cave.

She squinted toward the depths of the water in the corner of the cave and noticed that there was some sort of algae glowing in the darkness. She took a breath and opened her mouth to ask about it when she started to choke. Faster than Zelma had ever seen anyone move, Howlite appeared in front of her and placed their hands under her armpits to hoist her up above the water's surface. She gasped and rubbed at her eyes with one hand as she used the other to pull herself toward the shore.

"Zelma, are you alright? C'mover here," Daniel said.

Making her way toward him, she laid on her stomach on the sand, reaching out to place her hand on Daniel's foot. Daniel leaned over and intertwined his fingers with hers.

"I forgot not to breathe the water."

"I'm glad you didn't drown. Are you feeling better? You aren't even coughing anymore."

"Oh, yeah, I'm not."

Your body's different. You aren't a being of nature but of will, Howlite projected from where they laid on their elbows on the beach near Zelma.

You tried to make your lungs work the way they used to, but they don't have to. You can pull water in with your lungs or not, but whatever comes naturally to you now won't feel like breathing used to, Citrine thought.

I don't have to breathe anymore? Really?

No, you don't. That's why we didn't take you under immediately. We need you to be comfortable in your own fins before you can take the heat and the pressure at the palace.

Heat? Nevermind. Zelma shook her head and moved on. *So, if I believe I'm dead, I'm dead?*

That's too simplified, but yes. When we decide to pass on, our titles are passed down to new members of the pod.

Wait, I'm not the first Obsidian?

Nuh-uh. You are the second Obsidian. Now come back to the water.

"I'm going to try again, Daniel."

"Okay, I'm right here, waiting for the strength to brush my teeth and have a snack. Let me know if you're hungry or you need me."

"I always need you, but of course. I love you."

"I love you; I'm so proud of you."

She smiled at him, her heart in her eyes, before turning around and worming her way back into the welcoming lightness of the sea. Being careful not to expand her lungs, she sunk her body fully underwater. She tried to focus her eyes on the illuminated vegetation at the bottom of the cave when she saw it shift with movement. A rush of orangish yellow sped across her eyeline before slowing to reveal the shape of Citrine, smiling up into her eyes.

I'm so glad you made it into the water.

Thank you. Is that an entrance to the cave there?

Yes. The difficult entry is part of why we use this as a nursery for newer mermaids like you.

Are there many like us?

We're out here. Enough to fill the palace and maintain our territory.

I have so many more questions!

Ehy, Howlite, how about we make her a deal?

Oh, yeah? Howlite thought as both they and Citrine appeared seemingly from nowhere.

If she learns some of the moves we need her to, we'll answer some questions.

Sounds fair to me.

What moves are there?

Aht, aht aht, we are only answering this because it's part of the exercise, so don't get any ideas.

Shaking her head and projecting her exasperation in Howlite's direction, Zelma turned toward Citrine and cocked her head slightly to the left inquisitively.

You already drew out upon some of your magic when you authored the oath for Daniel and melted off those obsidian bonds—

Oh, those were made of obsidian, Zelma carefully projected as a statement.

Mmhmm, confirmed Citrine with her tongue in her cheek. *We are going to teach you some basic moves to help us protect you and give you a foundation for living underneath.*

Okay, but can we make the deal more specific to help me focus?

We're listening even—though that's a question.

Hush, Howlite. Yes, Obsidian?

How about for each move I learn, one of you answers some questions?

One question.

Okay! Deal.

So, the first move we're going to teach you is 'Call.' You were able to do it clumsily before, so you should be able to do it now. Your ability to imagine the ones you are Calling is key to how well and how far a member of the pod will be able to hear you.

Wait, I can control who hears me?

That sounds like a question to me, Howlite thought, as they circled overhead with the smooth movements of a dolphin.

Howlite, I feel like this one is pertinent to the move.

You'll spoil her.

Yes, you can imagine whom you want to receive your message and if they are capable, they will hear you. It's the same with hypnosis...

Enough show and tell, yeah? Face the sand and Call to us.

Zelma stifled the urge to pout and faced the large pile of sand where she could see Daniel's feet bobbing in the water.

Thinking quickly, she brought herself back to when she fell into the water at the statue. How afraid she felt as her bones melted and reformed. How much she would've wished to see Howlite or Citrine, or anyone, who could've helped her understand what was going on in that moment.

Howlite? Citrine?

She turned and saw their smiles and the light in their eyes.

Whatever you thought of did the trick.

Does that mean I'm up for a question?

Yes.

How did mermaids, or whatever we are, come to be?

Citrine and Howlite looked at one another briefly before nodding. Giving the impression of an exasperated sigh, Howlite locked their fingers behind their head and focused their milky white eyes on Zelma's.

Time to tell you a story that's been told by our kind as long as we've existed, Howlite projected.

Moving images began to flash through Zelma's mind as Citrine started to project her thoughts.

There have been many days and nights upon the Ocean and the Earth. On one such day, the Earth heard the cries of people being ripped from their homes and crushed into ships sailing across the sea to slavery.

The Earth said to the Ocean, "I heard these people cry out in tragedy as they were taken from me. Can you hear them now?"

"Yes," the Ocean replied. "Even now, they call out to be rescued, but no other humans are coming to save them."

"These people have been good to me, Ocean."

"They've been gentle to me, too, Earth. I'd like to prevent their generation from being wiped out. Shall we save them?"

"We're far too powerful. They'd be destroyed under our hands."

"Then let's create a being in our image to act in our place."

And so they did.

The top portion of her body was shaped from a woman that Earth remembered. A mother who, with foreboding, had braided seeds into her daughter's hair. A mother who wept bitterly when her daughter was taken.

And the lower half was formed from the body of a fish with strong, firm muscles and glimmering scales. The Ocean was confident a fish of its caliber could brave the hottest and coldest waters with ease.

Together they imbued this guardian with the power of a stone that would be the source of her abilities—tiger iron. She was the first of our kind. The first woman she rescued, Obsidian, was the second.

T-that's incredible. But I have so many—more—questions!

A deal is a deal. So, ready for the next move?

Okay, okay. What is it?

Block or Shield. Citrine, if you would?

Citrine summoned her focus before bringing her strong hands together with such force that Zelma felt a shockwave ripple through the water. Both of her forearms appeared to be made of citrine that was almost see through, and they glowed brilliantly with an inner light. She held her hands up in front of her, forming them into fists and taking a protective stance.

You aren't going to ask me to hit you? I really don't have much experience with fighting. Is that important underwater?

I wouldn't want to try Citrine, either, and I do have experience fighting. Knowing basic defense is important anywhere. You see her stance? Having a basic block could buy some time for us to get you out of trouble. Don't underestimate bluffing, either.

Okay, so how do I try this?

Conjure a strong emotion. Then, create an image in your mind of how you want to block and manifest it. Sing if you need to.

O-okay.

Zelma looked down at her hands. *A shield would be nice. It would have to be light enough to hold. And if it could cause some damage as well...*

Zelma brought her left hand up, wedding bands glinting as she closed her eyes.

In a rush of warmth, with bubbles forming around her, her hand was suddenly heavy with warm stone.

Citrine, that shield is decent, projected Howlite.

The shield in her arms was rounded on all sides and slightly convex. The rim was lined with obsidian that had been chiseled to a knife edge, ready to cut the clear water.

You'll need some training to use it, but it's a start.

I can't believe I can do this! Like, what am I blocking and shielding against? Why are you guarding me, for real?

There was a pause; Citrine and Howlite shared a glance before they swam a gentle circle around Zelma, and Citrine took over the explanation.

We aren't the only magical beings in the ocean—though numbers have been dwindling in the last century. It's not likely to be needed, but it doesn't hurt to know how to defend yourself.

There are also humans that might discover you or try to harm you. Also, some ocean creatures can be difficult to escape without hurting them. We can be killed or starved. However, we're very resilient and we tend to heal much more easily than humans, so don't worry too much, thought Howlite from her left.

This world is new to you, so you need the help. We are stronger together. Literally, our magic resonates off one another. Getting you to the palace safely is important to our sorceress and to us.

She suppressed the idea that there was more they weren't telling her and instead projected, *I can't wait to see others like us.*

They're hard to miss at the palace, Citrine responded with a gentle smile as she ran her hand the length of her floating locs.

Which brings us to what's next. We're going to find your affinity. There are three common types: Transformative, Healing, or Communications. We might not narrow it down this session, but anything you can learn about your magic will help you in the long run.

With a few simple tests, we'll see what you're naturally best at so you can train accordingly. The affinities are tied to your soul and your desires. The sorceress has mastered all affinities over time. Wait...

Howlite's expression soured instantly—like they'd smelled something offensive. *Agate is on her way.*

Citrine dropped her hands from her hair and trained her gaze downward intently.

Agate reporting in to give you two a break!

Agate is here? Another one of us? queried Zelma.

Mhmm. Howlite, go check her at the entrance.

Howlite didn't project another thought, but the look on their face could've been a curse word itself. They turned and swam swiftly down toward the glowing vegetation at the bottom of the cave. Their white scales glimmered in the dim light until they were gone.

I know you were going to teach me some more, but since it looks like we're going to be interrupted, I'd like to ask one more thing. Please, Citrine, Zelma begged and locked eyes with Citrine.

What was it?

You said mermaids are turned, but I don't remember anyone turning me or biting me like a vampire. What happened to me?

We... You... We can either be turned or be born, although being born a mermaid is incredibly rare in times like these and hasn't happened in a few decades.

51

Wait, so could I have been turned without realizing?

Citrine frowned in something like disappointment and Zelma felt utter confusion.

Agate at your service!

Interrupted by the arrival of Agate, Zelma turned her attention to the rippling water at the underwater entrance of their safe haven.

In a flash of movement, Agate sprung up from the water and threw her arms open in a semi-circle as she broke the surface. A cascade of droplets fell around her and glistened like sparkling diamonds. All over her body from her long straight hair down to the tightly laced corset that barely contained her chest to the scales at the top of her tail, were bands of pink, blue, deep maroon, and white. Even with the kaleidoscope of colors, nothing clashed with the neutral undertone of her medium-deep brown skin—a perfect composition of color.

"Hiya! I'm Agate," she said, as her high voice carried out the syllables in a singsong tone. "I was sent by our beloved sorceress to give your handlers a break. They're going to scout the area and see if we need to move you again before we descend. Oh, the human man! Hello!"

"H-hi," Daniel replied, nonplussed.

She's right. We're going to scout and head right back. Hopefully before Agate alters your hair forever... Howlite projected with a touch of pity.

Forever?

Agate turned her attention to Howlite and stuck out her tongue— silver piercing and all. Howlite returned the sentiment by placing their fingers under their chin and flicking them forwards with a look of annoyance and a hard thump of their tail before swimming off.

I'll remain in range as I patrol. Call me for anything, Obsidian, Citrine thought before nodding to Agate.

Zelma noticed that Agate didn't react to that last thought from Citrine. Focusing on only Citrine hearing her, she replied, *Of course. Thank you, Citrine.*

Briefly smiling in her direction, Citrine swam off to catch up with Howlite.

"I don't mind humans hearing me, though I know the traditionalists aren't a fan. Anyway, I have so many fun things in here!"

"In where?" Daniel asked, head cocked to the side.

"Here!"

Agate reached up and unsnapped a relatively large teardrop earring. Upon closer inspection, Zelma realized that the teardrop earrings, presumably made of some form of bright pink agate, were actually like miniature purses, complete with a silver clasp. Agate held the small stone in her hands and hummed over it. She clenched it in her palm repeatedly and gradually it began to grow until she needed two hands to hold it. Finally, it became so big, it began to float in the water.

"Obsidian, the look on your face! You've never seen magic on the surface, right? There's so much more than this."

"That *was* incredible," Daniel said from the small mound of sand.

"Thank you!" she said in response and, once again, drew out the syllables with that little singsong in her voice.

Daniel, be careful, Zelma thought toward only him. Disappointed, she remembered that he couldn't hear her as he leaned forward to inspect the purse floating toward him.

"Agate, what else do you have in your bag?" she asked pointedly, hoping to draw her attention away from Daniel. As Agate opened the bag, Zelma quickly shot Daniel a wide-eyed look—one they used with one another during family gatherings as a warning about certain relatives.

He nodded and crept back on the berm of sand, trying to appear busy organizing the cooler instead. The tension in his back betrayed the fact that he was listening to Zelma's conversation with Agate.

"I've got elixirs, exfoliators, serums, potions—everything. We can play around with the scales that aren't on your tail if you want to have an accent color. The tail scales are too resistant to change for the mild items I have with me; I hope you understand.

"Oh, yeah. I understand."

"Why not try my special relaxing whirlpool?"

"Aren't whirlpools dangerous?"

"You haven't tried my relaxing one, Obsidian. Oh, but first! Whatever you're wearing is not going to hold up to all the salt and heat of our underwater palace. You wouldn't want to be caught exposed if you're not into that sort of thing. Is it okay if you change right here?"

Zelma looked toward Daniel, who nodded, and she turned back to Agate and nodded back. Smiling, Agate approached, invading Zelma's personal space. She studied the zipper on the sandy black sports bra and smiled to herself. She unzipped it and pushed it off around Zelma's shoulders, exposing her breasts to the chilly interior of the cave.

"I have something that will fit you perfectly. Well, three or maybe six somethings, but I'll let you choose. Ignore that they're all white. I can change the color easily to blend in with those gorgeous black scales."

Suddenly, a tray floated in front of Zelma. It must have come out of the purse on its own. On the tray were five doll-sized tops. One was something like a bikini top, the next a bandeau. Then there was a bikini top that had a band underneath that would cover most of her midriff. There was also a top that appeared to wrap around itself and tie at one shoulder. The bottom of the garment had a ruffled peplum that would come down to where her scales began. Finally, there was a sleek-looking, long-sleeved garment that came with a hood and a mask that would shield her hair and mouth.

"Wow, did you make all of these, Agate?"

"Totally. I have more, but taking anything up to the surface involves a lot of finessing," she said as she vaguely pointed toward the bottom of the ocean. "I even have armor and more elegant wear in my shop, so whatever you choose now we can always change later."

"Thank you so much. Daniel, what do you think of these two?"

Zelma looked into Agate's eyes first and tilted her head and smiled when Agate nodded. With permission, Zelma grabbed the wrap-around top and the bandeau-bikini top and carefully swam over to where Daniel was sitting with his legs stretched out.

Carefully extending both palms, she showed him the outfits, being sure they were angled so that they were right side up to him.

"I'm honestly a little distracted..." he said. With a concerted effort, Daniel fixed his gaze upon the miniature outfits in her palms. "But... But I think I like the wraparound best. Especially if you—if we—are going to be meeting new people."

"I was thinking the same thing, although the other one is cute, too."

"That other one is your go-to swim top when you can't get your hands on a one-piece."

"It really is, though."

"In black it should be nice. I can't wait to see it," Daniel replied, leaning forward to brush his nose against hers.

"Mmm, I can't wait for you to see it," Zelma purred in response and pressed a quick kiss to his lips.

"Oh, young love. Should I turn away or should I watch?"

"No!"

"I mean, you could give us some privacy," he said, drawing out the last syllable and looking up into Zelma's eyes playfully.

"Daniel!"

"I'm mostly joking."

Zelma nodded and held the wrap top up higher. "I choose this one."

"Oooh, these are vintage now. I know you've already seen Citrine's armor and Howlites wreath, but there's so much more variation on what you can wear at the palace."

"That's nice to know. So, how do we get the top to be the right color and shape?"

"Well, first I take out a coloring agent. I'm thinking squid's ink. Where did I put that bottle? Oh, here!" she said, under her breath as she rummaged through her earring-turned-bottomless purse.

Uncorking a small bottle labeled in cursive writing that Zelma couldn't read, Agate set the ink on the little floating tray. Removing all the tops except for the one Zelma had chosen with a snap of her fingers, she carefully dunked the small garment into the squid's ink once, twice, and then three times. She corked the bottle after the third dunk and smirked to herself.

"Agate, you've done it," she murmured.

"Now, let's get this to your size."

She began to hum and stretched the fabric in her hands as it grew and grew. Before Zelma's and Daniel's eyes, the top had stretched so evenly that Agate could easily untie the shoulder of the top. With every stretch, the fabric seemed to breathe.

"This is like watching a magic trick," Daniel said breathlessly.

"This is literally a magic trick," Zelma replied with wide eyes.

"I love doing this for people who haven't seen me do this before. Now, arms up!"

Coming into Zelma's personal space once again, Agate deftly slipped the top over Zelma's raised arms and settled it over her bust. With a few pulls and tugs here and there, Agate was already fastening the top on Zelma's left shoulder. Reaching around Zelma, Agate pulled at the peplum in the back enough so she could create a point where the ruffles extended a little further in the back where her tail began.

"What do you think, Obsidian?"

"Wow, I think it's lovely. Truly."

"Daniel?"

"Gorgeous."

Zelma looked down at herself and couldn't believe how deeply black the soft fabric was, even where it hadn't been soaked by the water. It wasn't a greyish black, and it had no tones of navy blue whatsoever. Zelma was enamored with how perfectly the top fit, as if molded from clay around her.

"We have to add some sparkles. May I? I promise you won't look too much like me! I'll keep to your theme," Agate said with her face buried in her purse.

"Oh, y-yeah. That would be nice."

"I'm thinking rounded black ones for a subtle black-on-black look. They'll look just as shimmery above or below the water, I promise! Here, I found them!" Agate said, coming up out of her purse with another stopper bottle full of glittering, black beads.

"Yes! Okay, let's apply these around the ruffled edge," she muttered to herself as she took a quick handful of the beads and dragged her hand around Zelma's waist. "Mmhm. And here. Well, maybe a little pattern across your chest, too. Stop squirming! You'll ruin it."

Zelma couldn't help but wiggle around a little at having a stranger touching her so freely. Agate's palm brushed clinically across the undersides of her breasts. There was warmth and a slight tingle as the glimmering beads attached themselves to the top one by one. Just as quickly as she started, Agate finished altering the garment.

"Let's have a look, shall we?"

Pulling out a large mirror from her purse, she held it up for Zelma. She turned it carefully this way and that way to show off the gleam of the circular and teardrop-shaped glittering beads.

"You look so beautiful. You did such a good job, Miss Agate!" exclaimed Daniel.

"Thank you, Daniel!" Agate sang again, drawing out the syllables as she had before.

"Wow. I look good!"

"There is more. I don't know if you've realized it yet, but when you use your powers, there are certain markings that become more pronounced, like the lines around your eyes. Also, your lips may darken and your nails may become darker and appear more pointed. I can recreate the look so that it isn't apparent when you are channeling your magic. I was thinking something like this..."

Zelma watched herself blink in surprise as her face changed in the mirror. Her lips were darker at the top—almost completely black. Her bottom lip ranged from very dark at the outer rim to her natural brown nude shade in the center with a subtle wing at the corner of her lips.

They glittered as if they had been dipped in a shiny lacquer. Her eyes were lined in a sharp cat eye that followed the natural lines of her face. She reached up to touch her lips and saw that her hands had become slightly webbed claws. In shock, she looked down to adjust her wedding bands and saw that her hands were more human outside of the mirror's reflection.

"The mirror is only showing you an example of what I was thinking. I haven't actually done it yet. Would you like me to?"

She turned to Daniel, who smiled and shrugged. "Do whatever you'd like to do. You look beautiful either way."

"Okay, Agate. How do we do it?"

"Well, let's try this way. Remember that whirlpool I mentioned earlier?"

"Yes."

"Let's relax while we finish your look. I'll need you to lie on your back and float," Agate commanded as she hastily jammed all her tools back into her purse.

"Okay, and then?"

"Then I'll need you to close your eyes. I'll pour out these bottles in a circle around you, okay?" she said. She held up a trio of inky black and purple solutions in clear bottles. "The circle will cause the water around you to spin, and it will give you a calming sensation. The goal is to pull your magic to the surface and then capture that look and make it semi-permanent."

With a quick wave at Daniel, Zelma obediently closed her eyes and laid her head back into the dark, ocean water. Agate began to hum. Zelma kept her eyes closed while the water began stirring gently around her. Agate's vocalizations grew louder and more ardent. She dutifully kept her eyes closed and took deep breaths as the water began to warm and spin with urgency. Without warning, the sound of whales clicking and whistling echoed off the walls of the cave. Zelma threw her eyes open in alarm.

A look of horror spread across Agate's face as she reached for Zelma as if in slow motion. With a quick glance, Zelma saw that Daniel appeared to be asleep on the sand. When she looked down at her torso, she saw a hand, larger than any she had ever seen, with white-tipped stiletto nails wrap fully around her waist before pulling her down abruptly. She felt as if she were falling through space and through time. There were spots of light like constellations behind her closed eyelids. By the time she finished blinking, she was somewhere else entirely.

She was deep underwater, and the sunlight had faded. The bright water was framed by two large cliffs on either side. There were orcas, not just one or two, but at least a dozen. Zelma had trouble telling each of them apart by their markings alone. They circled her; they clicked and howled with anticipation.

Zelma was about to scream before remembering the way she had gagged on gulps of water just yesterday. She felt the pressure of the deep water against her ribs. She glanced frantically in every direction, looking for some way back to the safety of the cave where Daniel was, but there was nothing even vaguely familiar about the craggy cliff face or the whales that swam around and around in a way that disoriented her. She suddenly felt movement of the water underneath her, and the same hand from before was around her again, pulling her against a warm body in the cool waters.

Zelma was paralyzed with fear. She looked down and saw the belly and tale of an orca, but the abdominal muscles she felt under her back had her gaze dart upwards in a hurry. There was a woman, large enough to hold her fully on her tummy with room for another Zelma to spare.

Remembering her training, she pictured Citrine and Howlite as accurately as she could. She thought of Citrine's many bangles as they chimed together as she moved her arms and the milky white of Howlite's eyes, broken up by the black marbling around their pupils. More than any one detail, she recalled the safety she felt with them and how badly she wanted to feel that safety now.

Help! Please, help me! Citrine! Howlite!

Well, at least they've taught you something.

In just one projected thought, the impression Zelma got from the orca woman was one of absolute self-confidence.

Why did you take me? Who are you?

Ironic coming from someone who doesn't know who they are.

What? Zelma thought with a helpless shake of her head.

The large woman holding her smiled slowly, exposing two sharp canines among her unnaturally perfect teeth. *I have many names, but for you—call me godmother.*

Godmother?

That feels natural, doesn't it?

Zelma, in lieu of a reply, turned her gaze toward the pod of orcas still chattering and playing together.

I've taught my new pod some tricks. Their sounds are scrambling your attempt to Call the others. We wouldn't want anyone spoiling our reunion.

She pressed Zelma into her bosom, which was covered by some type of flexible armor with plates attached in black and white. Zelma looked up into her face. The woman's lips were a similar black to her own, but she wore eyeshadow—a stark white shimmer in her inner corners faded to a black shadow wing on both sides. Her skin carried a cool undertone beneath the deep brown. Her hair was long and loosely coiled, freely moving behind her as if she had freshly twisted it out. It was long enough that it fell to where her skin grew slick and taut as her tail began.

What is your name, hmm?

Zelma recalled the importance of a name and hesitated.

You can call me goddaughter if you'd like.

At least you are clever enough to know not to give your name. Good, Obsidian.

How do you know me?

There isn't a lot that I don't know—period. Come, goddaughter Obsidian. Fate is at hand.

She released her, and Zelma struggled to orient herself. The orcas, technically dolphins and not whales though they certainly could be killers, clicked and wailed to one another. Without delay, they began to close in on her and herded her south. As they continued to move, the cliffs seemed to close in on themselves and everything became darker. Her so-called godmother swam ahead of her, and Zelma could make out in the murky light that her top fin was much smaller than the others.

Come, come. It must be difficult for you to move quickly, but we don't have time to lose. That's it, follow me.

The orcas, acting as her godmother's shadows, kept Zelma hemmed in on all sides, steering her in the intended direction. With trepidation, Zelma took in as many details as the darkening waters allowed her to see. Zelma was able to make out the shape of bones on the ocean floor. Entire skeletons buried purposefully in the muck for decoration or warning.

As they swam even further, a cloud of the same inky mixture that sent Zelma down into this mess in the first place was swirling ahead. She tried to turn back, but the nudge from the snout of an orca pressed her toward where her godmother's body disappeared into the dark spill. Zelma could just make out the gentle wave of her tail fin slip into the other side.

She took a deep breath of salt water and tried to summon her magic. She thought of the shield she had made earlier, but the most she could manage was a soft, melting rock that slipped through her fingers like her chance to escape.

Dammit!

She was summarily nudged through the portal, where she found a large structure shaped like a giant's igloo with rounded cutouts along the walls. There were bioluminescent creatures dotting the building. Scarves of varying shades of purple were tied all around the structure, which held a loose series of interconnected platforms like floors. Some of the structure was partially covered, and other areas contained holes for plants and coral.

Is this really your home?

Of course, it is. I have a gift for you.

A gift?

I'm your godmother, after all. Better late than never, hmm?

Zelma furrowed her brow in confusion. The dome loomed large in front of her.

Come, Obsidian.

Instead of doorways, there were large open spaces in the structure. They entered through an exposed area at the top—her godmother confidently using her arms to pull herself through while Zelma lurched forward clumsily.

Once she pulled herself through, Zelma could make out shelves along the walls. The shelves held neatly organized bottles not unlike the ones Agate used for her concoctions. There was a topographic map on one wall, which was overlaid with light and kinetic symbols. There were stacks of gold coins and unpolished gems.

Zelma felt something crawling over her fingers. She suddenly noticed that there were little creatures cleaning the algae from everything. She immediately shook the tiny shrimp-like creatures from her hands.

You look more curious than afraid. Come down to the first floor. Don't you want to see what I have for you?

Without turning to look, the orca woman pulled herself down through another rounded opening in the floor. Seeing no other option, Zelma followed cautiously, pulling herself down into a room filled from ceiling to floor with objects. There was a set of ornate drums, overlaid with gold and pearls, that grabbed her attention. There was another hole, just to the left of the drums, that the larger woman swam through to the bottom floor. Zelma had no other choice but to follow her down. Along the ceiling in the final room were several portraits of her godmother, all depicting her in various states of undress. Hung up on the walls were a mix of swords, staffs, and other weapons Zelma didn't recognize.

The bottom floor was raised stone rather than the grey, thick sludge that coated everything else on the bottom of the ocean. In the center of the room, there was nothing but a pedestal. The room was large enough for the orca woman to casually circle her.

Uncomfortable being cornered, Zelma steeled herself and joined the woman. Like a dance, they swam in lazy circles, regarding one another in a moment that seemed to stretch from minutes into hours.

I shouldn't be surprised to see you so slow to act and yet I am.

I'm trying to understand what I'm seeing.

Understanding is what I'm here to give you. Step up to the pedestal.

Wait, understanding isn't something physical I can grasp—

Do I look like a simple turn of a phrase is beyond my intelligence?

No! You look intelligent! Zelma thought as she slowed her circling. *I'm the one who is not understanding what I'm here for. Can you tell me why you brought me here to give me this gift?*

Hmm, and if I do, you'll step up to the pedestal with less of a fuss?

What choice do I have? Yes.

Pausing, her godmother turned to fully face Zelma. Her presence was even greater than her size, and her powerful aura filled the room. With the pedestal between them, Zelma unflinchingly stared into the orca woman's eyes. She saw a cunning in those deep black eyes that shook Zelma's burgeoning confidence as a mermaid.

That sorceress—she had an opportunity to break necessary rules, and, as always, she only ever bends them to her detriment and the detriment of all our kind. I'll indulge your curiosity, goddaughter. I'll tell you a story —step up to the pedestal.

Okay, I'll accept a story.

Of course, you will. It goes like this...

The woman called godmother smiled and clapped her hands together. A wash of sparks and light issued forward and connected with the corners of the room, creating even more light. She then spread her hands apart gently, like a book, and there were holograms like puppets of light in the shape of the sun and moon over calm waves. Even with fear running like ice in her veins, Zelma felt compelled to lean forward for a better view.

As the woman spoke, the light moved along with her story.

The Moon, one night, pulled the tides higher than they ever had before and it delighted them.

"If only I had more time," said the Moon.

So, they asked the Sun.

"What could you mean by more time?" said the Sun. "Even when I'm out, you are still visible in the sky."

"But my magic is strongest when I'm alone in the skies. Imagine the strength I could build with more time! Maybe I would have power enough to drag the oceans across the earth!" said the Moon.

"No. I will shine as I always have," said the Sun.

"That's unfair. You are worshipped and revered more than me. I want to prove my power. Is there some time you are willing to spare?" asked the Moon.

"If you can gather more worshippers than I have, I will turn away from the earth and give those worshippers more time with you on those days that they outnumber mine."

Determined, the Moon began gathering worshippers from the seas. Together, the worshippers and the Moon would go on to eclipse the Sun, though never lasting long enough to realize the Moon's true power.

And that is the case today. You, goddaughter, Obsidian, have an opportunity to help eclipse the Sun—permanently. With enough time, our kind could be unstoppable. We could flood the earth and test our true power like the Moon.

But...wait, that can't be real?

It's more than a turn of phrase or a metaphor. It's the future. Our future.

You can't want to flood the earth, literally? Zelma projected with a hand over her heart.

The larger woman smiled slowly, as if just hearing the thought gave her great pleasure, before her eyes narrowed into a more serious expression.

What I don't want is to live a half-life in hiding. The days will not pass the Sun as they always have. I'm not the only one who sees this.

Her godmother charged at her. In an instant, Zelma felt a hand that spanned most of her back carefully directing her attention to the only furniture in the center of the ill-lit room.

You have listened to my story. Now, place your hands on the pedestal.

Shaking, Zelma complied. The center of the pedestal began to rise. Slowly, a life-size replica of Zelma's chest, midriff, and hips arose. The material was dark black, and Zelma instantly knew it was made from her namesake. Adorning this statue of her torso was a chain that ran around her hips and clasped through the statue's belly. The clasp was a rounded, golden sliver of what Zelma guessed was the sun and soldered at the corners to the silver moon piece. On the face of the moon was a round cut of a stone—a shimmering stone of warm brown with bands of golden mineral running through it.

Our history at your fingertips, goddaughter. You have no idea what the cost of this moment has been to me, her godmother said with an intensity that was almost hypnotic in how it echoed in Zelma's mind. *Touch the clasp.*

But...

Touch. The. Clasp.

Compelled, Zelma reached out and touched the stone that was warm to the touch. The chain unclasped and slithered up her arm like a snake. Horrified, Zelma jerked backward and bumped into her godmother's chest, which may have been a brick wall for all that Zelma could push back against her.

The chain, unabated, settled around her hips, and before she could move to pull it away, it bit her. The clasp pierced the flesh of the round of skin where her belly button would have been before resealing itself closed. Before the stinging of the piercing had time to fade into an ache, the larger woman quickly summoned a bottle and used it to draw another inky circle in the water between them.

Think about everything I've told you, goddaughter. This won't be the last time we see one another; I promise you.

With a mighty pull, the larger woman reached through the circle of ink as it grew more and more cloudy, and jerked Zelma through it like she weighed nothing—even with the drag underwater.

Half blinded by the ink, Zelma struggled and broke the ocean's surface. Her fin brushed something warm, and she splashed and threw her arms out with all her strength when she felt a pair of arms latching around her middle.

Obsidian! It's Citrine! You are safe now. I promise you.

Slowly, Zelma's struggles grew feeble, and she started to shake. She opened her eyes to discover the familiarity of the nursery cave. Her eyes darted to her right, and she relaxed that much more upon seeing Daniel groggily coming out of another deep, unnatural sleep.

She did something to me. Gave me this. I don't know what this is.

May I look at you, Obsidian?

You can, Howlite, if you come out of the water where I can see you.

Howlite's head instantaneously popped up out of the water, and despite her best efforts, Zelma flinched in Citrine's arms. Citrine made a vague, calming hum.

You! Stay there where we can see you, Agate, projected Howlite with a scowl.

"Where would I go? I told you I have no idea what happened to our new poddy!"

We heard you, Agate. Please, give us a moment, yeah?

Agate nodded where she was sullenly treading water, arms crossed, at the farthest end of the cave. There was still enough sunlight to see clearly, and Zelma couldn't help noticing that her earrings were missing.

She called me her goddaughter, Zelma thought as she focused on Howlite, who was reaching carefully for the clasp of the chain. *The woman who had me, I mean.*

Citrine blinked slowly and turned her head away with a sigh. *I'm going to let you go, okay?*

Okay.

Zelma carefully sat up and began stabilizing herself on the surface of the water with small movements of her tail that were becoming more natural to her all the time.

I think she told me to call her godmother in order to hide her name. It was some kind of game to her. But she knew me as Obsidian?

Citrine didn't respond mentally. Instead, she slowly reached forward to place a hand on Zelma's shoulder and bit her lip as if she were biting back words.

The first thing we need to do is figure out how to remove it. We've got to reach out to Sorceress Topaz, projected Howlite from where they had gently studied Zelma's new accessory.

"Z'ma. Where'd you go?" Daniel called from the sand.

Zelma looked tacitly to Citrine and Howlite and they split up—Zelma toward her husband and Citrine and Howlite toward where Agate was waiting on the far end of the cave.

"H-hey, Daniel," she called as she practically threw herself on the sand to be near him. "I was worried I'd never see you again. I love you so much."

"I love you, too," he said, sounding more awake the moment she touched his ankle. "I won't be away from you again."

"What do you mean?" she asked as she rested her head in the cradle of his legs. She rubbed up and down and noted that his brace wasn't there. She opened her mouth to ask about it when Daniel shook his head and looked across the cave.

He gestured upward for her to look to where Citrine, Agate, and Howlite had also turned their attention to an object projecting a hologram of a woman's head. The details were difficult to make out from across the cave, but to Zelma, it looked like they were in the middle of an intense discussion.

"I could hear Agate talking while I was asleep. I think they're taking you under."

"Under? Like, underwater? To the palace?"

"I won't let them take you without me."

"What are you saying Daniel? Are you sure you aren't feeling the effects of whatever happened to you?"

"No. I know what I have to do," he said and placed a shaking hand under Zelma's chin to stare deeply into her eyes.

"What are you talking about?" she asked, tilting her head to the side in confusion but still leaning into his gentle touch.

"I'm breaking the curse so you can take me with you. I just have to 'speak the secrets three' and I'm cursed, right?"

"No! That's too dangerous."

"What did you think I was going to say? If you disappear during our honeymoon, I'd have to live without you and try to pay bills without you. Hell, I'd have to come up with some story to tell everyone back home! I'm not going through that. I'm not going back on my wedding vows in the same week I made them! I'm going with you."

Heedless of the pressure on his knee, Daniel leaned forward and kissed her. Zelma felt the softness of his lips and her eyes grew hot with tears. She felt warmth drip down to her lips and realized that Daniel was crying, too. With a soft moan, she threw herself deeper into his embrace. For a few brief seconds, they shared the same breath, the same longing.

"I still don't think you should. We could get you out of here. I want you to be safe," she said between heaving breaths.

"Trust me. I trust you. It's your magic so I should be fine. I want to see you become everything you can be," he said.

"Daniel... Daniel, wait!" she ordered—only to have him cut her off.

"I believe that Zelma Cruz is actually the mermaid Obsidian."

At first, nothing happened, aside from the others snapping their heads around to look. Before Zelma could doubt that the curse had succeeded, Daniel was engulfed in a burst of blinding, golden light.

Zelma had to shield her eyes, and she was sure the others did, too. As the warm brightness faded, all that was left on the sand was a bottle. As she scooted over on her stomach to get a closer look, she realized that Daniel was in there, waving up at her on a miniature beach within the bottle. Carefully, she picked it up. Amazingly, he wasn't thrown around by the force.

What has he done? Citrine projected with a feeling of disbelief that tugged at the middle of Zelma's brows.

Hey! Hey, I heard her! In my mind!

Zelma's eyes darted to where Daniel was smiling like an idiot in the bottle.

Wait, Daniel, can you hear me, too?

Yes! Wow, you seem so worried. But look at me... I'm fine. Better than fine—my knee feels like I never fell!

What? You aren't in any pain?

No! I don't feel anything. The weather is surprisingly normal. Like a regular day. I don't even feel small except when I look up at your face in the sky. I could probably run in here!

To me, it looks like you fit with only a little room. This is impossible...incredible.

Citrine cut in. *Obsidian, I hate to interrupt, but we have orders to take you to our palace immediately. May I?*

Zelma nodded before she understood what Citrine was asking. She was shocked when Citrine placed her hands on the cork of the bottle and then, just as quickly, pulled her hands back to reveal a thin chain of delicate links made from citrine affixed to the bottle. She then carefully placed the chain up and over Zelma's braids and around her slender neck.

That should be easier for you to manage.

Thank you, Citrine.

Citrine nodded and turned her gaze toward where Howlite and Agate were waiting—matching expressions of annoyance and frustration written across their faces.

With a lurch in her stomach, Zelma turned her gaze down toward the direction of their underwater exit. With all of the loose ends tied up, she knew it was finally actually time to dive deep into the cold, dark sea. *Hopefully it's as welcoming as the poem says...*

CHAPTER 3
A PALACE IS WHERE THE HEART IS

*Z*elma! Can you hear me? Daniel called from the bottle affixed to her neck.

Obsidian! Citrine chided gently as she peered into Zelma's eyes.

Sorry, you were going over the plan?

You are going to follow us. We are going to follow the lights until we get to the opening of the cave. From there, we'll take a portal that will take us most of the way to the palace.

It's cloaked, but Sorceress Topaz is waiting for us at the front entrance, Howlite rushed to add before Zelma was distracted again.

Can they hear me? Because I can hear them—and you! Daniel projected, somehow loudly. Zelma looked down at Daniel, who was smiling up into her face, and then snapped her eyes back up to the others. Citrine had gently placed her hand over Zelma's where she gripped the neck of the wine bottle.

Sorry, Citrine. I'm hearing his thoughts and he can hear everything I hear. Is that normal?

There is no normal with soul magic; not really.

Did you hear anything about the descent plan? Howlite asked with a frustrated pinch of their stark eyebrows.

Oh, yes, but his thoughts are a bit distracting. I think I'm hearing everything from him.

It's your curse, so he's connected to your magic in this form. Focus on hearing us instead.

Oh. Okay. In that case, I'm ready. Daniel, I'll check in with you again soon, okay? I love you.

Y-yeah! I wasn't born yesterday, but I was born ready.

Daniel...

I love you, too! Go!

Okay, I'm ready to follow you guys.

Without another word, Agate and then Howlite turned their tails upward and disappeared into the deeper water below. Citrine motioned for Zelma to go next. With a last, unnecessary breath, Zelma pressed her palms together, straightened her elbows, and dived downward. She undulated her tail and propelled herself forward with clenches of her abs and pulls of her arms. She looked down to see Daniel relaxing on his back on the beach, watching their surroundings with interest from his new home in the bottle up against her chest. He appeared almost upside down, as the sand never shifted from the bottom.

It wasn't long before she saw the flicker of the bright, neon lights as they maneuvered themselves into a tunnel branching off from the belly of the cave. Feeling claustrophobia grip at her chest, Zelma summoned her courage and climbed into the tunnel after them. She was thankful to find the tunnel was wide enough for her not to feel the press of the walls against her skin as she followed them deeper and deeper.

The lights were evenly spaced throughout the tunnel, and a long moment passed where everything continued to look the same. Time seemed useless here, as there were only the muffled sounds of their movements. Zelma could just make out Citrine behind her if she craned her neck so that her chin was up against one of her collarbones. She doubted she'd have made a swim like this while holding her breath, but she supposed that was the point of the entrance to the nursery cave.

At the mouth of the cave, there was a large ring made from a smoothed, opaque, sparkling stone. The murky water near where the tunnel ended left a muddy taste in her mouth. It was hard to see to the other side with Agate and Howlite in the way. Zelma could make out that the hole was just large enough for two of the pod members to squeeze through together if they tried. On the other side was a mess of sea vegetation and plastic debris.

Where do we go from here? Zelma thought with dread pooling her stomach.

We go through the loop, Obsidian.

Are you sure we won't get stuck, Howlite?

We won't, Obsidian. Really, you won't. Now, place your hand on my tail and focus with us. Hum if that helps.

Zelma reached her hand forward, warily, and placed it up against a streak of black along the shining white of Howlite's scales. She was surprised by how warm they were under her fingertips. They all bowed their heads and hummed a gentle, somber tune. Through her closed eyelids, she could sense light building and sprung them open to see the band glowing.

After she shooed everyone back with her hands, Agate was the first one to fit herself through the opening. Zelma was shocked to see there was no sign of her on the other side. Then Howlite, who placed both their hands together in a diving motion, swam through with a burst of energy.

Zelma hesitated to even touch the brightly lit stone ring. She felt a warm hand and the touch of metal bangles on her back and turned to see Citrine smiling at her gently as she pressed her forward.

Much more carefully than the others, she slipped first one arm and shoulder and then the other through the band of stone and light. Before she had time to be afraid, she had pulled her tail fin through. She blinked when she emerged, as the ocean was much darker. Her eyes were adjusted to the near pitch-black darkness of the deep sea.

We aren't far now, thought Howlite, who, while not quite smiling, had a softer expression than Zelma had seen them have before.

Thanks. You—your eyes are shining in the dark!

So are yours. We're adaptable to the deepest waters, Obsidian. A human could never see, let alone survive the sudden pressure this deep.

Yeah, a normal human wouldn't, Zelma responded. She placed her hand around Daniel's bottle and felt his presence, if not any concrete thoughts, and kept moving. The thought that this was all real, that she was both Zelma and a mermaid named Obsidian, began to crystalize in her mind for the first time.

We need to hurry, yeah? Ehy, Agate! I didn't mean you. Don't go so far ahead! Come on. Citrine's already here.

She nodded and turned to see Citrine pulling her tail free from the hoop, which began to dim once she had entered through. Citrine pushed her along, and together they swam in a tight group in the direction Howlite and Agate led them.

They swam quickly enough that she felt the effects of the exertion even when she tried not to think about it. As they picked up speed, they moved low enough to the ground that the muck of the sea floor only just stirred as they passed.

Zelma caught flashes of movement. At the speed they were traveling, she could only take in the suggestion of a few deep-sea creatures here and there. The heat was growing and growing around her. Every mention the others made about the heat of the palace came back to Zelma as the deep red of what appeared to be a crack in the earth yawned open before them. Unsure of what was next, she shielded Daniel's bottle to her chest and felt the stirrings of panic. Could they really be swimming into lava? Was that something she, even as Obsidian, could withstand?

Before she had the chance to ask the question, they slowed and began to swim upwards and then stopped. One by one, starting with Agate, they pressed forward. Each one of them disappeared into nothing, just as they had before through the portal. Citrine, who had been behind her the entire way, came around and disappeared with a small wave. Hesitantly, she guided her fingers through the area where the others had disappeared. She felt a hand—warm and strong—grasp hers and pull her through.

Obsidian!

Zelma blinked and shook her head in sheer confusion. So many had projected at once that it was hard to make anything out except a sense of joy, a longing fulfilled.

Welcome home, Obsidian. I'm Sorceress Topaz and this is my palace. You're home.

Sorceress Topaz's voice, though she hadn't heard it in the human sense, carried an angelic quality to it. Her scales were a dazzling electric yellow-gold. She had on some type of layered robes that had a high collar and were threaded in gold. The robes were also bejeweled with her namesake stone, from collar to tail, and ended where her fins flared out. The outer robe floated around her, just as her honey blonde hair floated around her head. Her afro was perfectly rounded and coiled tightly enough that her jeweled accessories were kept perfectly in place. She wore a large, flat twist across the front of her hair where a crown was set delicately. Her lips were saturated with a golden, glossy color and her eyes lined with gold liner. The yellowy-olive undertone of her medium-deep skin highlighted the shine of each piece of jewelry she wore. Across her eyes rested an intricately detailed mask in yellow topaz and gold, tailored to shield the gentle curve of her nose and around her eyes where it winged out in a cat-eye effect.

Hello, Sorceress Topaz. Thank you so much, Zelma projected toward the sorceress and bowed her head. Almost instantly, Zelma again felt the touch of strong fingers—this time under her chin.

As she tilted Zelma's head up, Sorceress Topaz shook hers. *No need to bow. This is your home now. You have nothing to thank me for. I'm glad to see you here where you belong.*

There were many other mermaids milling around them. Zelma felt overwhelmed by flashes of different colored tails and faces and projections that flashed by faster than her mind could register. She clutched her head helplessly at the intensity. She felt as if she were in the eye of a storm of emotion, with heartache, joy, and curiosity swirling around her.

A crackle of electricity rang out as the sorceress held a hand high above her head. She gesticulated with her fingers in a motion that involved opening and closing her fist and pointing her fingers rhythmically. The silence was instantaneous, and Zelma was able to, for the first time since reaching the palace, concentrate.

Back, everyone. Those invited will reconvene in the meeting hall. The sudden travel is clearly too much for her. And who do we have here?

Realizing she was speaking to Daniel, Zelma carefully held the bottle around her neck up for Sorceress Topaz's inspection. The act brought Zelma back to when she was a child, showing her aunt a pretty rock she had found on the walk home from school.

What clever magic, Obsidian. Hello, Obsidian's lover.

Daniel waved happily from where he'd been poorly building a sand-castle on the white sands in the bottle.

Rarely is so much asked of us on a first curse, the sorceress thought as she released the bottle and straightened up. *This entire situation has been more taxing on you than I'd have hoped. But you are here now, and as sorceress, I am going to make sure we do right by you.*

There was a solemnity to the words the sorceress thought that left Zelma with the feeling that perhaps magic was being invoked rather than an empty platitude.

I—thank you so much. I feel like I've lived a hundred years in a few days, she replied as she felt the sting of tears welling up in her throat and behind her eyes.

Obsidian. You've borne so much. Please be patient for a bit longer and then you'll be able to rest a while.

I'm sorry, I don't know what to say. After what just happened with that other woman...

To see you chained, even ornately, is an insult to our heritage. May I touch the chain, dear one?

Oh... Yeah, of course.

As the sorceress reached forward to touch the clasp piercing her belly, Zelma felt another presence just out of reach of her ability to discern the scope of it. Behind her closed eyelids was some shadow in the shape of a woman, calling her by her new name. She flinched back before Sorceress Topaz could wrap her fingers around the large stone on the face of the moon. Alarmed, the sorceress cut her eyes to Zelma's.

Does it pain you?

No, but I think it... I feel like I'm going crazy.

You aren't, but why do you feel that way?

I think...I think it's alive.

That's not surprising, Obsidian. I have theories, but we'll save those for the brief meeting we're heading to.

Wait, now?

Unfortunately, but afterward you'll have some precious time to decompress before...well, you'll see.

With that thought, she linked her arm through Zelma's unresisting one and swam her into the palace proper. Before them were dome-covered platforms with rounded holes in lieu of doors or staircases. Everything was made from polished stone in every conceivable color and arrangement. Zelma looked up to see a dome that appeared to be made from glass that held some sort of duplicate of the sun. There seemed to be air inside the rounded top of the dome and within it was a tall kelp forest with hints of fish and other creatures disappearing and reappearing in the forest. The floor of the open area was a giant mosaic of crushed, glimmering stones arranged to connect all the different structures in elaborate paths of varying colors. The light of the small, model sun illuminated the entire outside area and glimmered off the stone paths.

They were headed to the largest structure, an expansive, tall ring of covered platforms not unlike the display of cupcakes Zelma remembered from her reception. The white opaque stone that the building was cast in gave the structure a shocking, ethereal feel amidst the dark black of the deep ocean. The water grew hotter the closer they came.

For the first time in a few minutes, Zelma remembered that Daniel was taking in the scenery with her. She looked down to see him giving her a thumbs up with both thumbs. Without taking too much time to focus in on his thoughts, she projected her feelings of fondness toward him.

By the time she brought her gaze upward, she was already being led into the uppermost circle of the strange building. Inside was a semi-circle of smoothed steps starting at the edges of the curved room and growing shorter until they reached the center. The walls were inlaid with intricate braids and twists of stone, which gave them a textured design that was unlike anything Zelma had ever seen. There were bioluminescent masses in transparent containers all around, with additional lighting issuing from the floor. There was fabric floating in delicate waves along the vaulted ceiling of the open room.

At the very center was a smooth half circle with an ornate frame behind it, not unlike a bed frame. It was in the likeness of a giant clam, from the cushioned seating to its scalloped edges. The stone clam was made of the same electric yellow stone of the sorceress' namesake. There were little details in blues and pinks that added texture to the front side of it. The flat of every stone stair had a plush, velvety fabric lining in shades of purple, while the fabric lining the bivalvia shape in the center was ivory. The ceiling was decorated with raw stone, like the inside of an otherwise dull rock with thousands of jagged, textured crystals. The stones were faceted with brilliant colors in a rainbow of shades across the room.

Come to the throne with me, Obsidian.

Sorceress Topaz had pulled her onto the plush seating at the center of the room. Zelma realized there were other members of the pod making their way to the stairs where they wouldn't so much sit as lay lengthwise and brace themselves with their hands behind their backs or under their sides. Zelma mimicked the position and found it to be much more comfortable as she wrapped a hand around Daniel's bottle and peered into the faces of the pod before her.

We are here today, June 5, 1998, to discuss Obsidian and the chain that has been forced upon her person. Aquamarine, are you prepared to take down the entirety of the meeting in the name of our pod under the rule of Sorceress Topaz?

Yes, Sorceress Topaz, responded a mermaid at the end of the row closest to where Zelma and the sorceress were laid.

She had her hair twisted into a thick goddess braid that wrapped around her head and, like a crown, was studded with teardrop-cut gems in her namesake. There were a few curls at her temples and the back of her neck that escaped the baby-blue braid. She was wearing a fitted corset of a porcelain-like material pieced together in shades of blue matching her scales. In her hands was a white stone tablet that held the gaze of her crystal blue eyes and contrasted with the deep brown of her skin.

Excellent. Spinel, are you prepared to guard the meeting and watch out for any intruders?

Yes, Sorceress Topaz, answered another mermaid who took a position near the opening in the back of the room.

Spinel had rounded bantu knots with geometric parts crisscrossing her scalp. Her scales were somewhere between ruby red and hot pink. From her wrists all the way to where her scales began, she wore some type of woven mesh with ruby-colored plates over her bust, down her spine, and on parts of her stomach. In her hands was a sharp-looking scepter that gleamed in the stone of her namesake.

Aquamarine, Spinel, thank you for your service.

Yes, Sorceress Topaz, respect to your name, the two projected in unison.

Now, assembly of peers, are you ready to carry out this meeting and come to a decision that represents our culture, our history, and the future of our pod?

Yes, Sorceress Topaz. We will honor our past. We will maintain the future of our people.

Let's begin. Agate, I'd like to start with your account of what transpired today.

Y-yes, Sorceress Topaz, of course, a nervous-looking Agate chimed in from her position in the middle of the gathered mermaids in the meeting hall.

I went to relieve Citrine and Howlite from their duty to give them time to do a sweep because of the reports of orcas behaving irregularly lately and because Obsidian is Obsidian, so... she started, pausing to glance at her scales and brush hair from behind her left ear, distractedly.

Please, Agate. Continue, the sorceress interrupted with the cadence of one giving an order.

Yes, Sorceress Topaz. I was dressing her and tweaking her appearance, as you can see. Then, I pulled one of my bottles. It was the squid ink-based elixir I always use. Only when I poured it... Everything went so fast! A hand with white nails reached through the whirlpool. Larger than I've ever seen one of us get. I am not capable of transportation magic like that on my own! Agate projected as she cast her gaze at the mermaids watching with a beseeching look.

Obsidian was pulled through, right in front of me, before I could grab her. I tried to Call, but there were orca sounds echoing off the walls of the cave. I think they made it so no one could hear me. By the time it went quiet, Obsidian was gone. I Called the guard back, but by then there wasn't much to be done. And now I'm the suspicious one! From then on, I had no more contact with Obsidian. I am here now giving you my honest recount of events.

Thank you, Agate, projected the sorceress with a cordial but not reassuring nod. *For the time being, you will be moved to the main palace. You will be interviewed further. Your materials will be examined, and the pod will help you create new batches of any of your products we find concerning. We, your peers, will render a final verdict regarding your loyalty as soon as these tasks are completed.*

Thank you, Sorceress Topaz, Agate thought with a sense of relief as she slumped into the plush velvet under her. In response, the energy of the room seemed to spike as glances and thoughts were exchanged between pod members too rapidly for Zelma to understand in the wake of the sorceress' decision.

Next, I'll call the heads of my personal guard. First Howlite and then Citrine.

Sorceress Topaz waved the two forward with a hint of warmth that Zelma hadn't seen in the sorceress' face since the meeting had begun. The two members of her guard sat up straighter and answered in unison.

Yes, Sorceress Topaz.

Howlite, please begin with your account of the events that led to the kidnapping of Obsidian.

Zelma flinched and clutched Daniel's bottle closer to her heart.

Howlite rolled their neck gently and then zeroed the whites of their eyes onto the sorceress'.

I began at the portal once Agate showed up to relieve us. There was a fishing boat coming in from the west chasing a school of fish toward the cave area, so I herded them in the opposite direction, yeah? With the fishermen minding the business that pays them, I briefly walked the beach in my human form with nothing to report. I heard Citrine Call for me. I made my way back to the sea and we discussed our findings. We returned to the cave when Agate Called us with the news that Obsidian had been taken.

Howlite has a human form? Do you think you can have one the next time you try? Daniel thought to Zelma.

She looked down at Daniel but was too afraid to answer. She just shook her head and held him closer instead.

Thank you, Howlite. Citrine, could I have your retelling now?

Yes, Sorceress Topaz, projected Citrine in response. She sat up and looked first at Zelma then the sorceress with an expression of regret pulling down the corners of her lips.

While Howlite investigated potential threats above water, I went below. I examined the stone portal at the base of the cave for any obvious tampering. I saw no indications of any change. I swam deep and found nothing, not even the human's machines trying to catch the pictures of the deep-sea squid. The location Obsidian was taken to was not near the safe cave. I Called for Howlite after my sweep, and we shared information at the cave's entrance. Then, we were Called by Agate to find Obsidian's lover asleep and Obsidian nowhere to be found. It was already too late...

Thank you, Howlite and Citrine. As for now, I have deemed your conduct appropriate. You may have a leave of duty if you wish to take one until the Welcome Ceremony for Obsidian. Should I need you for any more I will be contacting you at that time.

Thank you, Sorceress Topaz.

The sorceress nodded and turned her attention to where Zelma was seated next to her on her throne. Though she didn't appear that much younger than the sorceress, there was something in the older woman's eyes that made her seem infinitely wise—even larger than life. Zelma's heart almost skipped when the sorceress placed a hand—dripping with delicate stones—atop her bare one.

Now, customarily, Obsidian, you would be asked to give your testimony of events.

Zelma's eyes widened and she gave a minuscule shake of her head. All over her skin like a caress, she could feel the eyes of every pod member look her up and down.

However, seeing as you have not even been officially welcomed, nor have you had an opportunity to get your bearings in this life, I will seek your full testimony at a later time, and we will release that information as soon as is wise.

Thank you, Sorceress Topaz.

You are very welcome. However, in lieu of a testimony, I'd like you to swim in front of me here and allow a brief examination of your chain. Do you find that acceptable?

I... Yes, Sorceress Topaz.

Then I will need you to head to the front here. Thank you, Obsidian. Now, Opal and Pearl, please examine the chain and give us your findings.

Yes, Sorceress Topaz.

Two mermaids with deep, cool-toned skin and whiteish scales approached where Zelma was floating at the foot of the throne. Both had white, faintly colored hair, and upon closer inspection, eerily similar features. However, Pearl's scales reflected a soft pink light, while Opal had more of an iridescent tone to her scales and shimmery

85

rainbow highlights in her short afro. Both afros had a side part, but for one it was on the left and the other the right.

We were twins before we were transformed. Don't worry—everyone is always thinking it. It is a pleasure to meet you. And you, too, Obsidian's lover, projected the one on Zelma's left. *I'm Pearl.*

We wish the circumstances were different, though. Would you be comfortable with us touching you and grasping the chain to study it? I'm Opal, by the way.

Uhm, yes, you can.

Opal furrowed her eyebrows and delicately brought her hand forward to touch the stone that covered the silver moon of the chain with the coffin-shaped tip of a nail. Zelma flinched. It was almost like she felt the touch on her skin.

May we continue? Pearl thought with a question in her bright, milky eyes.

Zelma blinked hard as emotions and thoughts tried and failed to jump off the tip of her tongue—the edge of her thoughts. She opened her eyes to see twin intent expressions in the foreground and a blurred wash of the hues of the other mermaids, who were there watching the scene intently.

Yes, you may. I think the stone is alive. It's like the stone is trying to tell me something? Zelma asked, half hoping either twin would assure her that what she was sensing was normal.

Mmmmmhm, Opal projected.

Mhmmmmm, Pearl thought, echoing Opal. They appeared to be communicating something that Zelma couldn't decipher—even with telepathy.

This time it was Pearl who reached forward. Quickly, she placed one thumb and forefinger around the gold rays from the sun's side of the clasp and her other pair of fingers on the far side of the stone on the face of the moon's side of the clasp. She gently pulled and was unable to tug the clasp apart where the closure pierced through Zelma's skin.

It appears to have soldered itself together into one piece of gold on the side of the sun and silver on the side of the moon. The chain is made of finely braided tiger iron, and there are teardrop cuts of obsidian along each loop around the chain.

Tiger iron, Pearl? Does that mean...

Yes, Sorceress Topaz. It means that the stone is also tiger iron, and it resonates with our magic. Let us prove it. Obsidian, allow Opal and I to touch the stone at the same time—it shouldn't cause you any pain.

Okay...

Both twins touched one finger to the stone and hummed a wordless, mournful melody.

Instantaneously, Zelma felt the stone respond with warmth. The chain felt like it was a minute away from vibrating. Across her eyes— though they were wide open—she saw a vision of ships and lightning. A tingle of fear shot down her spine and pity pooled sickly in the bottom of her stomach. She threw her hand up to block her face from another flash of light, and her movement broke the connection between the stone and the touch of the mermaids before her.

Just like that, her eyes and her thoughts were her own again.

Obsidian? Are you alright?

I saw lightning, like there was a storm. There was a large wooden ship but then everything stopped, she projected. She shook her head as she felt flashes of wordless concern from the numerous pod members before her. *I think I'm feeling what the stone does—did? What is on me? Is there any way you could tell me? Please?*

Opal and Pearl nodded as one and turned to address the pod members at large.

As far as I can tell, this stone is tiger iron's stone—

87

Wait—just the stone? What about the person? Zelma interjected.

Obsidian, the sorceress chided. Zelma's eyed widened when she realized that the sorceress, as well as the entire meeting hall, was eyeing Zelma with varied degrees of annoyance and amusement.

Oh? Oh, I'm sorry, Sorceress Topaz, she projected in response, with a hasty bow of her head.

With a polite smile, Opal looked to the sorceress before continuing. *The chain will not be broken by our magic. There is a curse feeding off the power of the stone. Because it's tiger iron's stone, there should be enough power here to keep it clasped shut for a millennium. We'll have to nullify the magic to open the clasp and free Obsidian.*

Pearl, Opal, this has not happened in our recorded history that a stone has been left behind, Sorceress Topaz began with a pointed look at Zelma as she acknowledged her earlier outburst. *Nor has curse magic ever worked on one of our kind. Regardless of how likely there is to be a trap set for us, we must vote on venturing to the Abandoned City to nullify the magic of the chain on our Obsidian. To free her.*

Sorceress Topaz, respect to your name—could Tiger Iron have died in exile?

Spinel, be warned. This is still an official gathering, and you will speak only when called on to do so, Sorceress Topaz snapped in return, and there was an undercurrent of intense emotion in the silence of the large hall. *There isn't a way to know for sure without more information. I see that you had more. You may speak.*

Spinel nodded and replied, *Sorceress Topaz, with respect to your name. If we do remove the chain from Obsidian, could we not also destroy it?*

The sorceress nodded her crowned head toward Pearl to answer.

Theoretically, we could. Only something as strong as the thermal vent would be enough. But there is so much to study! Why would we?

Or it's some kind of curse that could affect us all further if it is left intact, Spinel projected back with a look of distaste twisting her features. Zelma felt her hackles rise. The ruby-colored mermaid looked her up and down as if she were the patient zero of curses. She concentrated in order to keep the thought to herself and filed it away to talk to Daniel about later.

Spinel, as one tasked with guarding the peace of this meeting, you are very close to failing at your one job.

My apologies, Sorceress Topaz.

Pod, who is in favor of heading to the Abandoned City to nullify the curse and to have the chain cut from our Obsidian?

Hands began to rise until the vote was unanimously in favor. Zelma hardly had time to take in the variations of jewelry and nail art before the sorceress commanded her attention once more.

Note that with the majority decision, we will have the chain removed. We will leave when the moon is highest tonight. Once this is done, we shall keep the chain in holding until after the Welcome Ceremony of Obsidian. We will reconvene to vote on what shall happen to it from there.

It is recorded, Sorceress Topaz.

Thank you, Aquamarine.

You are all at your leisure from here. I ask that you allow Obsidian and I our privacy.

The mermaids began to swim off into groups of two and three as they made their way out of the various exits in the meeting hall.

Oh, Obsidian! We would love to have you work with us after your ceremony.

We maintain and obtain magical artifacts and display some of them on the palace grounds. It's fascinating work, Pearl added to her sister's pitch.

You must have the constitution for having gone through everything you have with such poise, finished Opal with wide, hopeful eyes and a delicate, long-fingered hand on Zelma's forearm. *Sourcing magical objects can take you on quite the adventure. Not to mention what you've managed with your lover and that bottle!*

Oh, yeah, that sounds interesting. I'd be willing to learn more about that.

Pearl, Opal. Thank you, you may return to your posts.

Yes, Sorceress Topaz.

Respect to your name.

Before Pearl and Opal had cleared the room, the sorceress had looped her muscled bicep around the crook of Zelma's elbow and effortlessly led her in the direction they had come. She abruptly turned right and came around the back curve of the rounded, shimmering stone building.

Come, Obsidian and your lover. Let's discuss your retelling of events in the private of your chambers.

Oh? Do I have a room already?

You have always had a room at the palace.

Oh, is that because I'm not the first Obsidian?

Come, she responded instead of answering the question. *I'll show you.*

The sorceress led her to one of the only archways camouflaged into the outermost wall of the building. Zelma could feel the boiling heat of the vent along her back, and she turned her head to see the molten gash in the ground was close behind her. Fearing what could happen to her if she thought of it anymore, she firmly grasped Daniel's bottle and held it to her chest as she shifted her focus to the sorceress.

With a soft smile, Sorceress Topaz pressed her hand to the stone and hummed, the stone arch shape began to glow, and an emptiness appeared in the center of the archway. Zelma was gently guided through with the sorceress right behind her. The opening in the wall remained, but the heat of the vent diminished as they disappeared into the building once more.

The three of them were suddenly at the beginning of a hallway. This area had a roof that was curved and dotted with bioluminescent creatures moving slowly in a mimicry of constellations. The floor was a bright, softly glowing white stone, and they took a path to the left through a rounded hole in the wall. Zelma brushed her way through a curtain made of shiny, black beads that felt like obsidian under her fingertips and found herself in a room with rounded walls.

There was a pile of soft-looking, large pink bubbles of varying sizes clustered in one corner. There were also holes too small to fit through that functioned like pane-less windows where she could see red lava at the heart of the large vent in the earth. The centerpiece of the room was a statue, a perfect copy of the one she had visited as a simple newlywed on her honeymoon before everything changed. There was one noticeable difference, however. This statue was holding a curly haired baby, with the chest of a child and the tail of a fish. The statue was made of a mix of obsidian and yellow topaz, swirled and layered together to create remarkable shadow and complexity in the stonework.

Why is this here? Is this related to the statue on the mainland?

Yes. Intimately, the sorceress projected as she adjusted the rings and bangles before turning her back to Zelma.

Is that story about you? But how could it be, you seem so young.

You'll find that time isn't so strict on beings such as us, she thought before abruptly facing Zelma with an expression of determination where sadness had just been. *Obsidian, perhaps we should start with your retelling of events. All the information I receive will be helpful in freeing you and giving you and your lover the best quality of life we can. And the pod benefits, too.*

Oh, right. Well, I'll start with where I was pulled through the ink, because everything I heard today was accurate as far as I remember.

Zelma continued with the sorceress' encouraging nod.

I'm going to guess that whoever pulled me through was a woman. She was part orca, part human—a lot like us in fashion, but she was the largest person I have ever, ever seen. She told me to call her godmother.

Why do you think she would say that? the sorceress thought with a tilt of her head as she began to fiddle with the rings on the opposite hand this time.

Probably to avoid revealing her name? But she knew I was Obsidian. She calmed me down right after she pulled me through so I wouldn't drown. She and her pod of orcas, as she referred to them, led me to a building shaped kind of like this one.

I tried to Call, but the sounds the orcas were making interfered with anyone hearing me. I was scared. Her home, as she called it, wasn't as large as the smallest building here, but it was relatively similar in how it was made. She had whale skeletons and scarves and things decorating the outside.

There was a lot of stuff there I couldn't recognize. Some musical instruments and portraits of herself, uhm—half-naked. There was a statue with the clasp on it in the final room she made me follow her to. She told me a story about the Moon wanting to pull the tides across the earth and the Sun allowing it if there were more worshippers of the Moon. It felt like she was trying to indoctrinate me, but I didn't really get it.

I felt unsafe and as if I had no choice but to touch the clasp. The stone felt like it wanted me to rescue it, on top of everything else. It called to me as Obsidian, but I could be confused, because the woman was calling me to do the same thing, and it was hard to tell the difference between the voices at times. When I touched it, the chain slithered up my arm, down my stomach, and pinched shut through my skin. She was very bittersweet about it, and she touched the clasp one last time before sending me back through another ink portal.

Zelma looked up from the world of her memories to find that the sorceress had been doing more than mere fidgeting—she'd been weaving an especially thin, delicate chain of yellow topaz between her fingers as she listened.

That's an incredible amount of uncertainty and stress to go through so early into joining the sea. Oh, would you like to keep the bracelet I made?

Yes, Sorceress Topaz, thank you.

Would you hold out your wrist?

Zelma did, and the chain was carefully draped across her slender wrist and sealed together with just enough slack to be comfortable.

This is much better than the last chain.

Instead of laughing, as Zelma had intended, the sorceress' face grew more serious and those bright, electric eyes snapped to Zelma's.

You learn so quickly. You are everything I heard you would be and hoped you would be. I'm truly sorry that so much has been asked of you so soon.

Oh, no. It's fine, really, she thought and waved her hands as if to fend off the sorceress' growing sadness. Something about Sorceress Topaz felt so familiar to Zelma. Seeing her away from her duties as leader of the pod, Zelma realized that the woman before her was just a person, like any other, underneath the crown.

I know you have questions. I'll do my best to get those answered as soon as I get some more answers myself. Would you mind keeping these details private for now?

Of course, Sorceress Topaz. Actually, there is something I'd like to ask now, if I may?

I'll do my best to answer it.

Do…do you really think any of the mermaids in the pod are working with the godmother?

It was strange to Zelma, to see someone make the expression of a sigh without the gust of air. The other woman moved to lie against the pile of soft bubbles, and Zelma saw that those bubbles were the equivalent of a bed on land.

I don't want that to get in the way of you finding your home here. All you can do, unfortunately, is trust us.

But, Sorceress Topaz, honestly what do you know?

There are rumblings of discontent. You've only lived on the land above. Underneath, we've seen a decline in quality of life that has our pod passing on their titles earlier and earlier. Because of the need for secrecy, our numbers are lower than they ever have been.

Really? But why?

This is more than I like to go into with someone new, especially now... Sorceress Topaz thought as she got up and began to swim back and forth across the center of the large room.

Please? Zelma projected from the bed of bubbles, Daniel's bottle in both hands.

Sorceress Topaz faced Zelma before continuing.

There is much about your history that you have yet to learn. At first, we were in opposition to humans—we were created by the Earth and the Ocean to preserve a generation of our people that we were crafted in the likeness of. For years, we disrupted the slave trade and grew our numbers.

So, mermaids have truly existed for hundreds of years?

Yes. Over time, our pod has struggled within itself. We broke off from opposing humans officially in the reign of Sorceress Emerald. But technology and pollution have been making it harder to remain hidden than it had been. And with our numbers dwindling, a confrontation is likely to end with our magic being sold to the highest human bidder. But there are members of the pod who believe that confrontation is the only way to grow our numbers and live freely. Though I've tried to explain, I can no longer be sure who understands that the cost of mixing with humans could be our culture, if not our lives.

94

Wait, the Sun and the Moon and the Earth and the Ocean are real? Like, they have magic?

Well, no one left alive has heard anything but the stories. Either time is different for beings such as those or, well, no one knows what the alternative could be.

But if the godmother knows enough to lure the others and she had a stone... Does that mean she was one of us? Or did she capture one of the pod?

Obsidian, you are not on the royal guard. Perhaps you should rest while you can. You are a new pod member, and surely you need time to process everything you've seen so far?

I do, but... I still have so much I want to learn, Sorceress Topaz.

We are gathering intel on...the godmother, as you call her, but you are clever enough to have the same initial thoughts as I did.

Wait! During the meeting, I heard that Howlite has a human form? Do...do we all have one?

It's common enough. It takes firm control over your magic, and the farther you get from the pod, the weaker your magic becomes until you are essentially human. It can be quite dangerous, and many aren't as daring as Howlite.

One more! The most important question I have. When was I turned into a mermaid? How am I here? Zelma asked as she floated up off the pile of bubbles and closer to the sorceress in the middle of the room.

I-I can help you dig through the archives after your Welcome Ceremony. Obsidian, I will do my best to grant you more agency as soon as I can so that you can make your own choices. The same goes for your lover. There are ways to amend that clever curse you've designed. And there have been other tribes of magic people that include male members—perhaps we can try to rediscover someone who could help us get your lover mobile enough to live his own life on his own accord as well. This is just the beginning, I promise you.

I do have more questions...

Seeing as you are not keen to rest, come. There is one more place I'd like to take you before we reconvene for our trip to the Abandoned City.

Okay. But, Sorceress Topaz, what is the Abandoned City?

I'll tell you along the way. Come. You move beautifully considering how new you are, the sorceress projected as she once again looped an arm around Zelma's and pulled her toward the exit. *I doubt you noticed, but there are grooves and nubs designed into some of the walls. They appear decorative, but in actuality, you can grip them to help you maneuver or if you need to reorient yourself.*

Together, they made their way through the beaded curtain, down the hallways, and out of the large palace. Zelma hurried along as they headed the opposite direction of the vent behind the palace, toward the habitat-containing dome. There were other mermaids who waved or smiled as they passed but, likely due to the wishes of the sorceress, did not come any closer.

The Abandoned City is a smaller place we once used as a safe house. There was not always a central palace like I had built in my reign as sorceress. Humans have been encroaching on the deep more and more. Deciding the role of humanity and the role of our kind in the ocean has been the singular challenge to me as Sorceress Topaz, though it began long before my reign.

What did you decide to do?

Oh, sweet Obsidian. We are clearly in the midst of solving it still.

Uhm... How old are you? Respectfully, Sorceress Topaz, of course, Zelma projected with a wince.

The older woman cocked her crowned head and almost smiled. *We age differently. You have spent the majority of your life above water and away from the source of your magic, so you have aged as an average human. But now that you are home, you'll find that you age much more slowly. Our eldest members are from the 1920s. Most live a hundred human years; regardless of how you age physically, that's enough to inspire a soul to move on. When that happens, we have a Farewell Ceremony that will be much like your Welcome Ceremony. Our kind sleeps at the end of the Farewell, and they are swallowed up by bright, glittering light. They return to the magic that we all possess and free up their namesake stone for another.*

I heard that from Citrine and Howlite.

You are so determined to make up for lost time that you're trying to ask every question on the first day, hmm. Are you satisfied? May I continue telling you about the Abandoned City?

Yes, Sorceress Topaz.

So, the city, before it was abandoned, was used as a base. The city was built by a former sorceress in order to nullify magic—even our own— though we had methods of counteracting that, for our own sake. It was shrunk down and stripped the day the "city" was abandoned. There was a time when our largest threats weren't humans from above but fellow magical beings. You can see how having a mobile base like that would be advantageous in that case. Well, our scientists believe that if we get this chain there, we should be able to awaken its guardian and nullify the curse fortifying the chain. That way, we can easily remove it with no harm to you.

That makes sense. But there was one thing, Sorceress Topaz.

Yes, Obsidian?

The godmother. She said that it wouldn't be the last time I heard from her. Does she know about all this stuff as well?

Obsidian, we are prepared to protect you and free you at every cost. And we are efficient in calculating that cost and keeping it to a minimum. Do not worry for our sake or yours. I will answer more of your questions as soon as I am able to. For now, we're here.

Oh?

Turning to look behind her, Zelma directed her gaze upward, and up and up, to what appeared to be the sun shining over the top of a great kelp forest.

Oh, Sorceress Topaz, it's the sun!

We keep a habitat in our dome down here to repopulate animals and for our own gratification. This has been a kelp forest for a few decades now. What makes this one special, however, is the colony of cuttlefish that call this place home.

Cuddlefish?

Cuttle, and, well, they're often kind of angry. Most of them like to be alone. Some of them form little groups to hustle treats out of us. There are some paths through this garden leading to a stage at the center that we use for our ceremonies and such. We bribe the lot of them with a large amount of food so that they leave the guests alone.

They're capable of matching your scales to charm you into feeding them. There are other creatures here as well, but most of them tend to leave us well enough alone. We release some, and largely we have been able to monitor the population as ethically as possible. Hang out in the garden for a spell. Talk with your lover. My guard and I will prepare. We'll come get you, and we will go over the mission as a team.

Sure, I can wait here for a bit. Thank you, Sorceress Topaz. Really, for everything.

Of course, Obsidian. You are finally home now. And I will see to your agency and happiness. For both of you.

And with a rush of water, Sorceress Topaz took off back in the direction she had. Zelma looked down to find Daniel lying on his back on the miniature beach.

Daniel, are you sleeping?

Huh? Just resting a bit. I can hear everything. I don't get most of the emotional feelings you described, but even when you tried to suppress my thoughts, I heard things. I didn't want to interfere too much, though. I just listened, like TV, but I'm watching the world from the TV in the sky. How crazy, right?

Yeah, that's a word for all of this. So, you heard Sorceress Topaz say that we're going to do what we can to get you mobile again?

Zelma lifted the bottle right in front of her face to better catch Daniel's facial expressions.

Yeah. That made me feel a bit better... But... he thought, rubbing the back of his neck with his left hand distractedly.

But what?

You don't think she's hiding something, do you?

The sorceress?!

Yeah. She deflected a lot of your questions. Plus, she's randomly wearing a mask? And I feel like I saw the color of her scales when you first got pulled into the water...

There was that statue in my new room. But she says she'll have more answers, and I do need this chain off me. I don't think you are wrong, but you also weren't there when I was with the godmother. She was nothing compared to Sorceress Topaz. She was so unhinged, Daniel. I'm afraid to see her again.

I'm so sorry I wasn't there with you, Daniel thought as he rolled over onto his side and held his head up with his hand.

I'm glad you weren't. The way she talked about regular people... I think she wants to pull the land into the sea, Daniel. She thinks she's some kind of god.

I mean, aren't they, in a way?

Yeah, I have no idea what to believe about any of this. And no idea what she could be after besides worshippers or maybe time to gather them or something. It's hard to know if that story was actually a metaphor or if the Moon is "real" like the way mermaids are.

Yeah...

Speaking of what's real—what are our families going to think? We have, what, like two or three days until they expect to hear from us?

I don't know, Zelma. It's hard. Right now, we go along with everything to get the chain off you.

What about you? How are you, Daniel? Are you hungry or thirsty? Is it too hot?

No, he thought as he stood up and shook the loose sand from his sweats. *I'm not even sunburnt. If I wasn't more afraid of all the other issues we're facing, I wouldn't mind keeping this bottle around as a vacation spot.*

A new way of hitting the bottle, huh?

Exactly!

They giggled together and Zelma brushed at her eyes. If it weren't for the ocean around her, she was sure Daniel would've known she was crying a bit.

Oh, Zel—Obsidian! he thought and spoke at the same time.

Yes, Daniel? You know I can only hear you when you think, right?

I couldn't help it. The name thing is really important down here, isn't it?

Yeah, from what I can tell—it's a sign of respect for you and the others before you who have had that name. Everyone does it a lot.

I mean, isn't it science—that you should say someone's name often when you want to befriend them or sell them something?

Oh, yeah. That's true. Oh, hello.

It's a cuttlefish!

It swam by her in straight lines back and forth at her eye level, looking her over with the slitted eyes at either side of its head. Suddenly, the cephalopod began to flash colors, black and white and a few colors in between. The color changes happened so quickly they were hard for her eyes to fully register.

I don't have food, buddy.

She reached carefully toward it, and the cuttlefish pulled back its tentacles and fluttered the edges around its oval-shaped body. Thinking carefully, she focused on the skin on the back of her hand and shifted from deep brown to black almost as quickly. She held her hand near the cephalopod and they continued like that, flashing colors back and forth. It seemed to grow impatient with her when food was not forthcoming and disappeared grumpily back into the kelp.

That was so cool! What did it say, Zelma?

Huh? Zelma thought as she peered down into Daniel's waiting face.

Oh. I thought the color flashing was you communicating with it.

No, I was just copying it to see if I could. Apparently, I can.

Wait! If you can do that, do you think you're ready to grow your legs back like Howlite can?

You know me too well, Mr. Cruz, she thought, brushing her nose against the bottle affectionately.

I am your husband, Mrs. Cruz, he projected in return as he shook his face back and forth.

I do want to try to grow my legs back. But even if I could just walk out of here, I don't think it would be that easy.

You think you'd be able to give all this up?

To be with you?

I might give the world up to be with you...

We can't both give up the wrong worlds and be stranded apart.

You are what I refuse to give up, Zelma, Obsidian, Mrs. Cruz, my love.

Yes, yes, I feel the same. Whatever world gives me you. God, I wish I could kiss you.

Me too. This kelp forest is just the perfect date spot.

What if I try this?

She lifted the bottle floating before her and brought her lips to the glass, pressing a kiss to it with her dark lips. She pulled back and was shocked to see that there was no transfer. With a small laugh, she remembered that this was magic and not regular, human makeup.

Daniel was still standing up with his arms out as if he could hug her lips and kiss her back.

I hope seeing your giant lips like this doesn't awaken something in my sexuality...

Daniel, you're too much! Seriously. But we won't have to awaken too many new things in our sexuality if I can transform back to a human to have sex...someday, she thought with a pout blossoming. *First, the chain, then getting you back to normal, then me back to normal, then our lives back to normal... Whatever we want that to be.*

Yeah, a new normal.

Yeah—

Obsidian. It's time. Howlite and Citrine are coming to collect you and take you to the front of the palace, projected Sorceress Topaz.

Zelma's eyes cut away from Daniel's and her head turned around as if she could pinpoint the source of the sound.

Yes, Sorceress Topaz. Thank you!

You are welcome, Obsidian. It looks like your range is improving already.

Hey, Obsidian.

Startled, Zelma turned around to see Citrine emerging casually from the kelp.

Citrine! I thought you were going to be on leave.

I don't like loose ends. Plus, I'll have time for leave after your Welcome Ceremony.

Thank you. I do feel better having you around.

Hmmm, Citrine projected with an expectant look.

What?

I'm just waiting for questions of some sort.

Don't we have to get going? I'd love to know more about you, if you're offering, though?

Yeah. I'd be willing to answer some questions for you real quick. Did anyone call you nosy up on land?

Zelma looked down to see Daniel nod until he caught her gaze, at which point he shook his head with a wink in Citrine's direction.

Zelma rolled her eyes. *I suppose a few people. Knowledge is power. And I find people interesting.*

Hmm, Citrine replied, her expression unreadable.

So, before we leave, can you tell me a teensy bit about how you were transformed?

It's not much to tell. I had a big family. I worked near the beach, cooking at the pier. They called me fat, stupid, you name it. Day after day. I could have fought back, but I chose to dream instead, even in the daytime. I started to see the shapes of women in the water beyond the pier. One morning, I skipped off the prep for the fish fry. I walked to the end of that pier, I climbed over the railing, and I let go. I thought I was going to meet god before the sun rose, but I met the women in the water first. They brought me to the palace, and there I found my purpose.

Citrine... I'm glad it all turned out well, but I'm so sorry, Zelma projected and resisted the urge to place a hand over Citrine's.

Please, save your concern. This happened decades ago. My life now is more than anything I could've dreamed then. You'll see how it is.

I'm sure I will...

Are you both wasting time?

Howlite! Zelma projected. She was startled to find Howlite right behind her as if they'd always been there. *Citrine was telling me how she was turned.*

That's a story worth wasting a little time. But you know how Sorceress Topaz gets. Come on, I'll trade you a few details about my story if we swim and talk.

Yes! Thank you, Howlite.

Yeah, yeah, Obsidian, they projected as they led everyone out of the dome and toward the entrance of the palace.

So, I was kicked off a cruise ship. I spent most of my life blending in as masculine or feminine as I needed to be, so most of the people on the ship thought I was a man at that time. I was something of a con artist—only to those who could afford it! There was some gambling, drinking, you know. I was after the code to a vault, and someone's daughter thought she was in love with me the same night it came out that I was a stowaway. I ended up passed out drunk in a rowboat someone pushed out to sea.

Oh, Howlite, that's horrible! Zelma chimed in with a hand over her mouth.

It wasn't ideal. I thought I was dead, but before that happened, I was found by what I thought were angels. It's hazy, but I know I called them all sorts of flattering things as they put their hands on my boat and pulled me to an island. They threw water and other helpful things onto the beach, and I crawled back into the water after them. I feared dying alone. The life I have now is one of the few things I didn't have to take and now my life is mine, truly.

Wow, Howlite. Did you want a hug, too?

A fist bump is cool for me.

Of course.

Maybe we could come up with an original handshake sometime during training.

Yeah, I'd like that.

Perfect. You've arrived. Now, let's go over our plan.

Zelma did a double take. It dawned on her suddenly that she'd followed Howlite to the entrance of the palace without realizing it.

Yes, Sorceress Topaz.

Seeing as Obsidian has yet to attend her Welcome Ceremony, she is the most vulnerable of us all. However, seeing as we are given no choice but to escort her to the Abandoned City, Howlite will lead, as this a stealth mission above all else. Zelma will be in the middle with Citrine. The rear will be taken up by Aquamarine and Spinel, as they are also valued members of the royal guard. That's a team of five. The fewer of us in waters populated by larger amounts of humans the better for staying hidden. That's why I am considering joining and making this a two-team mission with only Obsidian and I...

Sorceress Topaz. You are the author of the rule you are suggesting breaking. Surely that's not necessary! Spinel projected with a raise of her ruby eyebrows.

Sorceress Topaz, with respect to your name, you are vital to the future of our pod. You cannot venture up from the palace short of an emergency. Waking the guardian at the Abandoned City, even risking a trap, isn't anything we can't handle, Aquamarine projected as she placed a hand on Spinel's shoulder.

Aquamarine, Spinel, thank you for your input. The reason I am considering this is because we are all aware that the...the godmother, as she's called herself, is likely doing this to gain attention from me. She knows of the Abandoned City, and this is most certainly some sort of ambush. I am powerful and likely more powerful than her, especially if I take her by surprise. We cannot look at this as a mere retrieval mission for artifacts.

Sorceress Topaz, it is not the old days when you first became sorceress, with respect to your name. A display of power like that could draw the attention of humans and what then? Having to remain hidden hampers the most powerful—that obviously includes you.

Spinel, that is enough. Fellow royal guard members, what are your opinions?

Respect to your name, I agree with Spinel, added Howlite.

I also agree, Sorceress Topaz. We can handle this. We have a teleport ring here and there so it shouldn't take much to get home without being ambushed or seen, Citrine chimed in. *Allow us to serve our purpose.*

The sorceress was still for a long moment before she nodded. *I'll be requesting updates. I will be right by the portal should the need for me arise. At this point, we need to teach Obsidian the basic hand signals we use to supplement the projections.*

Holding up a closed fist, the sorceress looked to Obsidian.

This is stop.

She changed her fist to an open hand.

This is come. You can still nod or shake your head for yes or no for now. If you flash your hand open and closed, it means danger. We have many more, but that should do.

Are we aware of techniques that woman might use? thought Spinel, with a toss of her head.

We are aware of her using the orca's calls to disrupt our projection signals. The size of her tail makes it difficult for her to lay low around humans, Howlite supplied.

If she chooses to stay hidden from humans. What says she won't force our hand, Sorceress Topaz? Spinel answered.

I am confident that if she were going to expose us all to humans, she would have done that without involving Obsidian.

I suppose, Sorceress Topaz.

She should be treading carefully. She does teleport without stone, however. That will likely be her play. You will have to stay tight and make your way to the center of the city where you will awaken the guardian to nullify the curse on the chain and break it.

Sorceress Topaz, what about Daniel? If his curse is undone with him in a bottle like this... Zelma interjected and cradled Daniel's bottle to her heart.

That could happen in a worst-case scenario. We are more than capable of helping him breathe underwater momentarily, but he would likely have to go back up to the surface if the curse is nullified, Citrine projected, not unkindly. *We should be able to do that before he runs out of oxygen.*

But what about us, Sorceress Topaz? What if our magic is nullified?

That's what these medallions are for. The sorceress clapped and enough medallions for each of them appeared in her hands in a flourish of light. *Touch it and manifest your stone in the empty space in the center. This should fortify your magic and render you immune to the effects. Our enemy doesn't have access to these so, while it is possible she has developed other means, at the very least we will be evenly matched.*

Okay, thank you, Sorceress Topaz, Zelma thought as the group began to pass around the medallions.

You're welcome, Obsidian. Remember, your job is to stay with the group and avoid any attempts to separate you.

Yes, Sorceress Topaz.

Sorceress Topaz furrowed her brow in concentration as she summoned a small, stone hoop from nothing. Gradually, she stretched the hoop until it was as large as the portal Zelma remembered at the entrance of the nursery cave.

This is the portal that ties to the Abandoned City location. I'll be waiting. You'll be fine, Obsidian. I promise you.

Sorceress Topaz held her empty hands above her head, and the heavy-looking stone hoop she'd summoned held itself at eye level for the group. With more grace than Zelma had thought possible, Howlite pulled themself back before expertly swimming through the hoop in one stroke. When it came time for her turn, Zelma delicately put first one arm then one shoulder and the other through until she emerged in a different part of the ocean. Howlite was looking back for her and pulling her along. She looked back to see Citrine emerge and catch up immediately, followed by Spinel and Aquamarine.

All through. Now the Abandoned City should be straight ahead. Stay in formation, Obsidian.

Yes, Howlite. Of course.

I'm not the sorceress; you can be less formal if you'd like.

I can't help it at this point, Howlite, respect to your name.

Good, you can still joke. You'll be fine. Your lover, too. I'll see to it.

Thank you, really.

Here it is up ahead, Citrine called.

Oh, I thought calling it the Abandoned City was a play on words, but there's even statues of people and small buildings, Zelma projected to the group.

It was built by a previous sorceress. It's modeled after a place that was dear to her. Let's get on with this. Not only could your godmother be lurking around, there are occasional divers that like to admire the ruins as well, Spinel projected.

It's crazy to me that the divers are as dangerous to me as her.

You'll get used to it, Howlite replied.

They approached the model city that was roughly the size of a football field. There were various statues of citizens and buildings the size of a child's playhouse in various stages of ruin. There were no doors or windowpanes on each of the ten buildings organized in a loose semi-circle that Zelma could count, with at least as many statues of adults as there were smaller, child-shaped statues.

In each of these buildings is a flat panel of stone. We use that with our hand flat on it to wake the creature temporarily. We must split up to hit as many panels as possible at the same time to create a surge of magic strong enough to wake the creature. There should be just enough of us that it won't take long.

Yes, Howlite, chimed the group.

Zelma felt as if it had dropped to the tip of her tail fin. Faintly, but drawing closer, was the now familiar sound of whale calls.

Before Zelma could think of a hand signal to use, Citrine swung a muscled forearm out to latch on to the crook of Zelma's arm. She motioned with her head, and Zelma followed immediately into the nearest small building.

Surprisingly, the small building held enough space for Zelma and Citrine to pull both their tails into with enough space not to feel cramped. Citrine's eyes widened. She pointed out the window behind Zelma.

Unbelievably, the unmistakable bubble of an oxygen tank caught Zelma's eye. Disappointment flashed through Citrine's face, and she gestured for her to crouch down.

Divers? Why now? Zelma asked rhetorically.

Horrified, Zelma realized that the orca sounds were blocking Zelma's projections. She thought briefly about spelling words out in obsidian but realized they probably didn't have the time for that.

Citrine must've sensed her panic because she placed her hands on Zelma's shoulders and nodded encouragingly. She pressed her into the corner of the building and held up a fist before leaving carefully out of the doorway and sealing it off behind her with stone. Zelma looked closer and realized the stone sealing the doorway appeared to be a raw, unpolished form of Citrine.

The bubbles that accompanied the scuba divers seemed to move on quickly, but before any true relief could settle over Zelma, the floor began to swirl with telltale purple-black ink.

There is no way she's going to fit in here!

Not fully, no. But halfway should be enough room for us to reunite, goddaughter Obsidian.

The woman who called herself her godmother was halfway into the room phasing through the floor through an open portal. Her head was high enough to have to crane her neck to keep from bumping into the ceiling. Unlike at her lair, her eyes were drawn as if she were in pain. Although the water was murky, Zelma didn't doubt what she saw—the woman cornering her was weary.

Help! Citrine, Howlite!

They can't hear you this time, either. I thought you more clever the last time we met. Could've been a fluke, I suppose.

What do you want?

I told you—I just wanted some time with you, goddaughter.

Aren't you worried about being seen?

They're already getting to you, hmm?

What do you mean?

Why should we hide? Why shouldn't we take our rightful position as deities?

You say that and yet you're hiding in here with me, godmother. You chained me for a reason, what was it?

Zelma stared up into the eyes of the woman looming above her. Without her adversary's tail fully through the portal and exhausted looking as she was, her godmother was less imposing. She felt the stirrings of bravery deep in her heart until the other woman narrowed her eyes at Daniel's bottle. Zelma quickly curled her fingers around it and held it protectively against her chest.

Your lover looks scared—perhaps you've found one of the few sensible humans there are. How dare you demand anything of me when I'm just trying to help you.

Daniel, can you hear me?

Y-yes. This must be her?

They turned to take her in, their eyes traveling up and up to see where she braced herself in the small building with her elbows almost up against the ceiling with only the flat stone counter between them.

Yes. Can you hear the conversation?

I think so. I love you, if I never get the chance to say it again...

Save your goodbyes for another time, young lovers. If the humans who love to track my pod of orcas so much hurt you or them—in any way— they will be the ones issuing tearful goodbyes.

Zelma narrowed her eyes and cocked her head before she could stop herself. Carefully, she inched forward toward the counter.

Don't look at me that way, goddaughter. I have great plans for us. Can you believe they tried to take a copy of my voice, along with the orcas, with one of their machines? We are mere experiments to them, when we should be so much more.

So that was your plan? Use the whales and the humans as a distraction?

This is just the start, Obsidian. I know you feel helpless around me. But what about the humans? You felt the same way with them, didn't you? Even though you were one of them just last week.

I—well...

The larger woman was breathing heavier as she craned her neck to regard Zelma further. *All of us feel the same way with things being as they are. We cannot continue like this. I am far from the only one that knows this. There must be a reckoning, and it might already be too late in history for it to go as far as it needs to go. We need more time, and I'll see to it that we get it.*

If it's too late, why try to change things now?

Because time is malleable. Reality is malleable. I will be the one to shape it for the good of our kind if no one else will step into that destiny. I will be the Sorceress of the Moon, and I'll bring an end to land as we know it.

You're obsessed with pulling people into the sea, Zelma returned and eased herself that much closer to the counter. She flexed the muscles in her arm in preparation.

Or pull the sea over the lands. Either way, really, she smirked.

How could you think that murdering so many innocent people is—

Innocent people? I'll transform those who are willing to follow! We shall have the upper hand until this earth sees fit to end—and that will be a lot longer under my rule.

What do I have to do with this?

I want you to join me, Obsidian. You have such promise, goddaughter. With you in the palace, I can get the upper hand over Sorceress Cowardess and take my rightful place. Oh, don't look at me that way. Many of our kind see me as a visionary.

I'd never join you. What you're doing is wrong! I don't know how you don't see that.

Oh, so when the sorceress pulled you back into the sea it's fine, but when I want to pull other humans into the sea for the good of our kind—it's horrific? Your mother is the same hypocrite she has always been.

W-what?

There was a tense silence as the women maintained eye contact, frantically trying to read one another.

Even now she hasn't told you who you are?

What the hell are you saying?

Did you think I chose the title goddaughter out of nothing? Everyone at that mediocre palace knows. You are wearing my stone—the stone of the first of our kind. The position of sorceress was stolen from me by your mother. And here I am in exile while she prepares to throw her daughter whom she stole back into the sea a party! Imagine throwing a ceremony while the future of our kind grows bleaker by the day. Mmm.

That can't be true.

Now, bring that stone to me. As usual, there isn't much time. I only need to touch it for a moment!

Zelma leaned in and, before she could think twice, raced forward and placed her hand on the countertop of stone between them. It lit up in response.

Her godmother released a screech of rage and whipped out a hand to grab at Zelma's midriff—placing her palm across the stone. Instantaneously, thoughts and feelings from the stone swarmed Zelma's mind. She realized that she had closed her eyes and threw them open quicky to see that her godmother was radiating new energy. The briefest contact with the tiger iron decorating the moon side of the clasp was enough to revitalize her.

Y-you don't know what I sacrificed for this moment and the next. I shed my own tail for this revolution.

113

She collected her thoughts and stopped short before she continued as the stone under Zelma's palm lit up even brighter.

Everything I do is to restore order to this world! Help me and further the strength of our kind for the greater good.

Never! L-let go of me! Let go of the stone!

There's never enough time...but there will be!

Suddenly, they both looked to where the citrine sealing the doorway began to melt. There in the doorway stood Sorceress Topaz, looking furious. To Zelma's horror, her intricate topaz mask was missing and in its place was a face with an uncanny likeness to Zelma herself.

Another time, Sorceress Cowardess.

Without another word, Zelma's godmother threw herself downward and back through the portal at the floor of the small building. To Zelma's immediate relief, the room felt instantly less cramped the moment her ink began to dissipate. In the moment of silence afterward, Zelma felt a late burst of adrenaline hit her bloodstream as she whirled around to face the figure at the door.

You lied to me, didn't you? You're my mother! Like in the story! I don't want to believe her, but tell me it isn't the truth.

Obsidian...

Tell me you didn't let me think my mother was dead all these years? Zelma projected as she lunged toward the doorway.

Obsidian, I'm Howlite. I'm definitely not your mom.

Zelma could only blink as the appearance of the sorceress melted away, leaving the familiar features of Howlite in its place.

Is—is this why you're always on the stealth missions? Zelma projected in an attempt at levity.

Yeah, it is. Obsidian, I can't answer anything for you that the sorceress should. For now, we gotta use this time to get to the front of the city. As soon as we woke the creature and I hadn't heard from you, I guessed that Tiger Iron got to you. Citrine managed to herd the orcas away while avoiding being seen by the humans, and the humans were following the whales. This is our chance to reach out to the guardian.

Shaking, Zelma looked down at Daniel and briefly smiled at him. She nodded and followed Howlite through the maze of algae-covered stone until they reached a small crawl space under the front of the city. Slowly, she became aware that a creature was crawling forward out of the dark and through the muck. As it got closer, it looked like some sort of dust mite she'd seen pictures of in school, only much, much bigger.

This isopod was once large enough that the city would fit on its back, and that was how it became mobile. But as magic has waned over the years, it has shrunk to a more manageable size.

It's still taller and wider than me... Zelma thought, flinching backward slightly.

Well, you're about to be more creeped out. It's going to cut the chain with its mandible.

Oh, come on.

Holding still, Zelma felt her atoms trying to fly apart as the creature grew close to her. If not for the charm around her neck and her intense focus, she had no idea how she would've been able to exist at all.

She flinchingly shuffled toward the guardian's mandibles. The creature obligingly reached forward and, with the quickest of snaps, the silver portion of the chain that looped through her skin was cut. Not a scratch was left on her. The chain remained hugged around her waist, almost as if it were clinging to her on its own.

Gingerly, Zelma reached down to touch the tiger iron and felt the warmth of it in her hands as Citrine pulled her backward and the creature burrowed back under the ruins of the Abandoned City.

I'd like to keep it around me for now. It's not pierced through my skin anymore and that's what matters, right?

Sure, Obsidian. Let's head back while we can, Spinel called before turning toward the direction of the stone hoop they arrived through, waiting, suspended, for them to return to the palace.

Realizing that she'd forgotten to check in with Daniel for some minutes, Zelma craned her head down to see Daniel looking back at her with compassionate, warm eyes. She smiled briefly before swimming faster to keep up with the others.

As they hummed the hoop to life and swam through, one by one, all Zelma could think about was the conversation she needed to have with Sorceress Topaz. Citrine tapped her shoulder, and with a start, Zelma realized it was her turn to fit through the stone hoop. Without wasting another second, she darted straight through.

The palace loomed large ahead of them as they approached the answers, hopefully, to her questions.

CHAPTER 4
AN ENDING IS JUST A NEW BEGINNING

With a speed Zelma hadn't realized she possessed, she undulated her tail frantically. She was the first one to clear the barrier that hid the palace from the outside world. She shook the feeling of déjà vu as she saw the sight of Sorceress Topaz, masked once again, there to welcome her as she had been the day Zelma first arrived.

Welcome! I was so relieved to hear from Spinel that the chain has been cut. Obsidian, this is just the beginning of me keeping my vow to you and your lover. I'm sure we can—

I can't believe you!

Obsidian?

*Sorceress Topaz, we ran into—*Howlite started to project from where they and the others were clearing the barrier themselves.

Into my godmother, Zelma interrupted. She gulped around the burning lump of tears in her throat. The others seemed to fade into the background.

It's time you told me the truth, Sorceress Topaz, Zelma projected as she reached forward. Zelma carefully and deliberately pulled the mask away from the older woman's face.

The sorceress made no move to stop her. Instead, she merely looked away. *What did she say to you, Obsidian?*

You can't even look at me, Mother. You already knew what she'd try to tell me!

Obsidian.

And how would you know what she could have said if it weren't the truth?

Sorceress Topaz, please allow us to excuse ourselves, Aquamarine interjected.

Y-yes. Please do. We will continue this in Zelma's quarters, thank you.

In the periphery of her vision, Zelma could make out the faces of other mermaids. Most of whom hadn't gone on their mission to the Abandoned City. They were staring openly, peering at her with varying degrees of curiosity, pity, and sympathy. Some of the heat of her anger dimmed into a dull ache of embarrassment. Aquamarine carefully handed the sorceress the medallions, and Zelma, seeing the hand off, hastily pulled the charm over her neck, angry but careful not to remove Daniel's bottle as well. With little fanfare, the sorceress disappeared the charms and turned to face her daughter.

Come with me, Obsidian.

Zelma flinched back as the sorceress reached for her arm.

Please, Obsidian. Just...please.

Giving in, she linked arms with her mother and swam with her toward the largest structure, down the secret hallway, and to the room that must have always been hers.

Tucking the beaded curtain in behind her, the sorceress steeled her expression.

May I have privacy with you, Obsidian?

We are in private.

118

Your lover is glaring at me.

Anything you say to me can be said in front of him, Zelma said, crossing her arms with Daniel following suit.

Obsidian! You're acting impossible to deal with!

You're acting like a compulsive liar.

I'll let you have that last one, Obsidian. Do you even want to hear anything I have to say at this point?

Yes, I really do, Zelma replied as she lowered her arms.

What did that woman tell you?

I'll tell you that after you tell me the truth. I wasn't turned into a mermaid like most of the others, was I?

No, you weren't turned.

No! I was born, wasn't I?

Zelma's voice, even in her own thoughts, wobbled with the weight of the anxiety and pain they were projecting back and forth to one another.

What happened to me? Why did I change back?

Y-you know the poem. You mentioned it earlier and I thought you knew then.

Zelma swam back and forth slowly as she processed the new information.

The poem was about me. Your father and I. I had been thinking about humans and what to do as they developed more technology and destroyed more and more of their world and ours. I was trying to come up with an answer in those caves, far away from the palace, the day I met your father. Instead, I found love and had you. Until I didn't. I had to leave that cave without the loves of my life or an answer to the question that's been plaguing our kind since it was decided we would go into hiding.

What happened?

That's the second of my regrets. One day when you were small, you were playing with your father on the beach, and you manifested legs to take your first steps to him. At first, I was excited; mermaids are not often born to term. I had to live on land in those caves for the duration of pregnancy to be sure you developed with enough oxygen, in case your human half needed it to develop properly. So, when you manifested your magic, I was thrilled. I put too much hope in bridging the gap between mermaids and humans in my love with your father. But, after that day, you never changed back—no matter how deep into the ocean I took you. Your magic never manifested in any other way. So, I handed you over to your father. And then I was called away to handle some matters at the palace for an extended time...

And then my dad passed away and I went to live with my aunts...

I had no way to find you. I set up that statue and planted the story in the minds of a few humans that lived on the islands. The story spread. I hoped that the ocean would call you home. And it did! You're here, before me. You're so beautiful. I shouldn't have lied, the sorceress thought, turning her face away to wipe at her eyes and hold her head in her hands.

Why did I transform at the statue?

That statue was created to sense my bloodline. As soon as you returned, I made my way there. I have the power of telekinesis so...so it was simple to pull you into the water with me. You were so terrified, and I was afraid I'd drown you, but when I touched you and willed you to turn, your magic responded to me as a woman in a way it hadn't when you were a baby. You began to change and then my guard portaled in behind me. I returned to the palace, and they monitored you until it was safe to bring you home.

They were both shaking as Zelma lifted her mother's chin with two fingers to gaze into her eyes, desperate to find validity in what her mother was saying.

Our scholars have been able to make some theories on the onset of puberty in relation to the awakening of feminine magic. We don't fully understand, as there are so few pregnancies to study. And if you forgive me, I'll leave this life with only one other regret.

With a sigh, Zelma leaned forward and grasped her mother's hands in hers. The only sounds were the gentle chime of the sorceress' bangles and the muffled sound of water.

And Tiger Iron or the orca woman, whatever her name is—she is truly my godmother?

Yes. She saved my life when I was human, though she was Tiger Iron then. She's the reason I am Sorceress Topaz now. The former sorceress, Sorceress Emerald, chose me as her successor despite Tiger Iron possessing the stone of our greatest matriarch.

Why?

I'll never fully know. Tiger Iron, at her core, wanted to remain a goddess among men. I fear she is escalating to tangible actions rather than of her usual, distractable bitterness. She never wanted to hide what she is. She longs for worshippers above and below the seas. The former sorceress fostered a kindness for humanity and hoped to resolve things peacefully with my reign. So far, I have failed her. Tiger Iron exiled herself when I was chosen as sorceress, and I have only heard rumblings about her since.

But she found me so easily.

You must be important to her plans against me.

Why did you forbid the others from just telling me all of this?

We are creatures of will, Obsidian. I didn't know your constitution. I feared you might despair and that maybe your magic would respond and leave you. Rather than see your stone and your title passed on too quickly, I kept the truth from you. I wanted to be sure you were able to bear it. I had already lost you once... I see now that my grief clouded my judgment.

I don't think that's a good enough reason.

I doubt you will. Please do not take your frustrations out on my guard. They are loyal and good, and they kept secrets from you out of those motivations. Citrine was especially concerned with how you'd react.

I could do that.

Well, Zelma? You have your truth. What will you do now?

I don't know. The stone is still here and alive. I have Daniel and now a pod of people to get to know. Maybe we can come up with something to do about Daniel and our families?

We can get started on something for that after your Welcome Ceremony tomorrow. As for the stone, we'll have to put that in our archives for further study.

It shouldn't be destroyed, Zelma thought as she rubbed at the chain still hanging low on her hips with a will of its own.

I didn't agree with that motion, either. Seeing as you are curious about it, I can allow you to have it until we begin your ceremony at the next moon. Before your ceremony begins, I'll have Pearl or Opal pick it up for you. I think you'll love seeing the archives for yourself.

Not as much as Opal and Pearl will enjoy showing me around.

Both women laughed away the last of the lingering tension in the air.

May I address your lover?

Zelma looked down to where Daniel was back to calmly sitting up on the beach. At his thumbs up, she turned her gaze back to her mother's.

Yes, looks like he's giving you permission.

You've been the only one that can hear him because you haven't learned to manipulate your projections and the projections of humans. Our magic is especially effective against souls aligned with masculinity.

What? Oh, can you both hear my thoughts at the same time? Daniel thought.

Yes, we can for the moment, the sorceress agreed as she leaned forward to hold his gaze.

This is not how meeting Zelma's family on the mainland went... Oh, I mean Obsidian!

You can speak freely. I gave her that name, after all.

I knew you were hiding something! You two do look so much alike...

I was just going through so much at once that I missed the obvious, Zelma thought grumpily.

As soon as your godmother said it, I knew it was true, Zelly.

Yeah, I did, too, Zelma replied, turning her attention back to her mother.

I hate that you found out from her rather than from me. I often think when others act. Which is why, with one of my life's regrets resolved, I would like to ask both of you to help me resolve the other. The time is coming when humans will be at the front of our palace. Even now, the cloaking we use to hide is becoming obsolete in the face of human technology. With you both, maybe we can develop a strategy to counteract this inevitability.

I don't know exactly what I could do to help, but I want to try.

Me, too! Daniel chimed in.

Good.

Oh, there was something that my godmother said that still worries me. She implied that there are others that agree with her ideology in the palace.

I am sure there are. I can be certain my guard and a few others are trustworthy, but beyond that all I can do is offer a solution they could choose instead and work toward the goal of pulling everyone onto the same page.

That's just a lot to think about.

You also have your Welcome Ceremony. Even now, we are commissioning decorations, fun foods, and a performer—the most popular of our generation. His name is Atlas, he's a percussionist. Most of the women lust after him. He can transform from dolphin to human, and he has quite a hold on our pod especially, the sorceress added from where she'd gracefully laid back on the pile of soft, resilient bubbles.

Wait, there are that many other types of magical beings?

Of course, though many have assimilated or gone extinct. One lead we could follow to get Daniel more mobile would involve reconnecting with a tribe of seahorse people who may be willing to lend their expertise on the matter.

I could be half seahorse? Daniel asked in shock.

Does that mean you'd be the pregnant one if we had babies?

I mean...I mean, for our family...I could?

The mother, daughter, and son in-law shared a laugh.

You two are so sweet. I hate to see you separated as you are. I promise you, I won't hold back anything from you any longer. I should have trusted that you'd be as strong and kind as your father.

Hmm, I want to know you more, Mother. I'd love us to have time to get to know each other, but I am going to need some time to process everything.

Oh, yes, absolutely. I'll leave you to your thoughts until later when we'll prep for the ceremony, Zelma's mother said as she elegantly lifted herself up and headed for the door.

Oh, okay, Sorceress Topaz.

Okay, beloved Obsidian.

With a soft smile, she was swallowed up by the hallways of the largest building in the palace.

Well, that went better than I thought, Zelma projected to Daniel. She held his bottle up toward her face to get a better look at him as she spoke.

Yeah, it did. Ehy, Zelma?

Yeah?

What's that other curtain go to?

Zelma turned her head in the direction Daniel was facing and realized that, on the wall behind the statue, was another beaded curtain. She shrugged and used the decorative grooves and grips along the walls to orient herself in front of the curtain. She hesitated and shared a giggle of suspense with Daniel before aggressively pulling it open. The beads slowly floated back into place behind them as Zelma glided through.

Oh, I should have expected it to be something like this, Zelma thought with a tilt of her head.

Me, too. But I'm still surprised.

The bubble bed was one thing, but a bathroom? she thought as she twirled around in the center of the room to take it all in.

Well, there's no toilet.

You know, I haven't had to eat or sleep or... The other things, since I transformed.

But I thought you slept at the cave with me, though?

That was only after I was mentally tired. If I don't feel tired, then I'm not.

Daniel merely nodded until his expression shifted into something mischievous.

What, Daniel?

What happens if you think about peeing? he thought. She turned to see him giggling where he sat in the sand.

I don't even want to know at this point.

It's kind of been nice—not worrying about those things for a little while. I hope I'm not backed up when I get back to normal!

Ewwwww! Zelma thought as she giggled.

Hey, I can't help but think about stuff like that...

Why don't we take your mind off that? There's gotta be some cool stuff in here.

I can't believe this room is so big when there's only, like, a window, a vanity, and a mirror.

Zelma looked up to see a section of the ceiling where clothes seemed to hang on their own. *Hey, there are also clothes up here. I guess you aren't used to looking up at the ceiling for some extra space.*

I guess not. Wow.

I probably have stuff I should be studying or doing.

I mean, you do, but maybe you should play around with some of the clothes and magic makeup stuff. I'd love to see it on you.

You know I barely wear makeup because of work. I'm out of practice, Zelma whined.

She blinked and watched Daniel stand up and shake the sand off his hands.

I know you have some fun when you do. I heard everything that, uh, my sorceress in-law said. Maybe we should have some fun for at least a few minutes. I can't play with you in the ways we usually do. No board games or making out to get your mind off things. I know you are strong mentally and I doubt you'll just fade away if you get too stressed, but— why not release a little bit of steam?

126

Relaxing is probably good. I just feel like if I go too slowly, all these thoughts will hit me at the same time. I just want to keep moving... Yeah, you don't have to look at me like that. You're right.

What I would give to kiss you right now.

For saying you're right?

As rare as it is that I am right, you would think so, but no. I just love you. My amazing, brave, strong, playful wife. Seeing you like this has me falling more in love with you. When I met you, I knew you were going to be big in some way. I can't believe I get to be your husband.

Zelma was sick of crying, but this time she didn't bat the tears away as she held the bottle so carefully with both of her hands.

Daniel. I love you, too. It means so much to me to hear you say that. I'm not going to leave you in that bottle for long, I swear to you. You've sacrificed so much to follow me here, and I will do everything in my power to keep that from becoming a regret for you.

It could never be, so you win.

It's torture not being able to hug you.

Let's try on some clothes and check out the kelp garden for a bit. Then we can rest here until the ceremony starts.

That sounds great.

So, what do you think about this one...?

She reached up and pulled down the first item of clothing she touched. Down came a cloud of sheer black fabric with a thick, fluffy, boa trim gently pooled around it.

Wow, that robe is certainly a look, Daniel thought with a hand gently rubbing his chin in thought.

Everything in here is black, she thought as she leafed through a few more of the tops hanging above them. *I'm trying this one on first.* She slipped first one arm then the other through the large robe that seemed to shrink and writhe around her until it fit perfectly.

Hmm... It looks good on you.

I feel like I'm the wealthy, newly widowed woman coming to the door to answer questions from the paparazzi.

I mean, it's not bad, though. As long as I'm not dead in that scenario, I'm cool with it.

You could be the pool boy who moves in later that week.

What else do they have in there?

A few outfits that are mostly strings, something formal looking, like a tux coat, and a bunch of wrap tops.

I don't think there are any rules against nudity here.

I know, right? I like the mood of this robe actually. I kind of want to wear it out.

Then do it!

With a twirl that set the robe around her to spinning, Zelma sped over to a wall that had an alcove displaying at least a hundred bottles on a semi-circle of small steps.

Let's see if there are any fancy bottles I can use. Oh.

What?

I can't read any of the labels. They're not an alphabet I understand.

Hmm, that seems a bit ominous, but I think we have to at least open, like, one or two. For science.

I knew you were a bad influence on me, she sighed. *Here, let's try this mint bottle.*

Delicately, Zelma picked up a clear bottle filled with a mint-colored solution with an ornate top made out of a type of sea glass. She hesitated for a second before carefully pulling out the stopper with a pop.

Wow, are these bubbles? Daniel thought as they watched them begin issuing a dozen at a time out of the small bottle in Zelma's hand.

It's a lot of bubbles. They smell minty, Daniel.

I guess you have to get clean somehow? Unless they are candy?

I'm not eating these! The bubbles aren't stopping on their own. Oh, how am I going to get the cap back on?

Try willing it back on while you press down...? Maybe it works like a magical childproof cap?

With a considerable amount of force, Zelma shoved the stopper back into the bottle just as the next round of bubbles was about to join the others floating toward the ceiling.

Barely did it. Wow. My hands feel cleaner, though.

I bet another one of these bottles is toothpaste!

I'm not opening another one of these without mermaid supervision.

Where's the fun in that?

C'mon. The fun is going to be in the kelp gardens with the cuttlefish.

I suppose some "fresh air" will do us good.

I have to ask—you said it's nice in there. How's the air?

It's been great. The water is really clear where I can touch it, too. No other animals or anything. I'm pretty sure the tree is fake, even though it feels real enough to me.

Wow, Zelma replied as she wound her way through the hallways of the building and made her way toward the courtyard.

I think the kelp gardens were that way, Daniel thought, pointing out a path on the left.

Oh, you're right. How did you know that?

The crushed stone on the floor. It's color coded, I think. The green and yellow pieces lead to the kelp garden.

That was a really good catch, Daniel.

Well, I have an interesting view from in here. You notice more of the world when you're just inches tall.

Obsidian!

Oh, hello, Pearl and Opal.

It's good to see you out enjoying the palace. Everyone has been especially curious to meet you.

With a suddenness that shocked her, there were mermaids popping their heads out of different structures. Some held back and peered curiously at her, but a startling number were heading over to join Pearl and Opal, gradually forming a loose semi-circle around her and Daniel.

Oh, everyone. Hello!

Welcome!

Woah, Zelma thought as she placed a hand to her head. *There's so many of you.*

Everyone, one at a time, Pearl chided.

I'm Aventurine, thought a mermaid with dark green eyes. Her hair was a shade of auburn and twisted in short twists that curled out from her head in every direction.

I'm Tektite! projected another pod member with dark, blue-black scales and twin afro puffs coiling above where the rest of her navy blue hair was slicked to her scalp.

Jade here! another mermaid thought. She wore a bright green garment that covered her from her hair to her wrists. Her tail was the same brilliant green with hints of almost white dotted along her scales.

I'm Jasper! yet another mermaid chimed in. Like Agate, her scales were not a solid color but banded with many different hues of red and blue and white. Her head was buzzed, and her smile was warm and kind.

And you remember Spinel and Aquamarine.

Everyone, let's just save the rest of the group's introductions for tomorrow before and after the ceremony, yes?

The slew of mermaids swam off in various directions in a cacophony of colors and smiles and waves until only Pearl and Opal were left behind.

I hope that wasn't too much. I know speaking to large groups can be taxing when you first learn the skill. It gets easier, though, Pearl added with a soft grin.

Thank you. Hey, I'm sure you both are on your way to attend to something, but how do things work around here? Like, in the daily life of the palace? Zelma couldn't help but ask.

Well, right now a lot of us are grouped in our committees prepping for the coming ceremony. Generally, we have festivals for other reasons. We host talent shows, sparring events, music, and other art showcases. In between that, we work on skills informally with one another, attend meetings, and form committees for maintaining the palace. We grow stronger together and care for one another. There are also some rescue teams that help animals and occasionally humans that we may be able to turn.

This seems like how the world should be, Zelma projected.

It's not like it is in the upperworld. We aren't expendable to one another. That isn't to say there aren't differences. But, in our history, we have largely worked through those differences. Between you and me, that woman is a different case, however, Opal replied.

It's frustrating how many are tempted by what she's saying about the upcoming confrontation with humans, thought Pearl.

Pearl, Opal, you don't believe she's right about the future of our kind?

Hmm, Pearl replied first. *I like to believe that we have more time than we think to find a solution without labeling any of us expendable in the process.*

Yeah. I think we need more minds and more time. I can speak for both of us when I say I'd love to work with you. We haven't been to the surface in decades, and we could use a fresh perspective like yours.

I'd love to help, though I'm not sure how helpful I can be. I'll try my best.

Excellent. Citrine is going to be so disappointed when you are on our committee first instead of training.

Wait, there's training?

You shouldn't have even said anything, Opal.

Opal smirked and nodded her head in the direction Daniel and Zelma had been headed. *We'll let you head out to the kelp garden. It's beautiful, isn't it?*

Yeah, thanks. I can't wait to talk to both of you more.

Of course! Bye, Obsidian!

Bye, Pearl and Opal!

That was a fun talk, Daniel projected.

Yeah. No matter how many questions I have there are always, always more.

That's just how you are—adorably, annoyingly inquisitive, Daniel replied as Zelma followed the stones toward the large dome that housed the kelp garden.

Says the kid who got his tests handed back face down.

Okay, we aren't going to do this. School isn't built for learners like me.

You know what, you're right, love. Even though you're a troublemaker, you learn so much better when you get a chance to work with something.

132

You're so smart, and I couldn't cope half as well with all of this without you.

Thank you! Daniel replied with vindication echoing the thought.

Zelma distractedly patted the bottle. She peered up at the replica of the sun through squinted eyes and the tall, swaying stalks of kelp.

We're here. They mentioned a stage, but I never got far enough in the kelp forest to see it.

Well, let's go find it then.

Brushing past the first few spindly stalks of kelp, Zelma made her way to one of the few winding paths that took her deeper into the calm of the kelp forest. As big as the dome appeared to be on the outside, it was nothing compared to how small it made her feel as she wandered to the center of it. At the corners of her vision, she could see hints of tentacles and flashes of colors from the cuttlefish rife in the forest.

That must be the stage. Its build is in the same style of the half-circle-shape meeting hall, only much higher up.

I guess so the person performing can be seen? Daniel asked.

It looks like there are some mermaids setting some things up on the stage...wait. Do you see that drum, Daniel? The gold trimmed one with the pearls? Zelma projected toward him, her heart skipping a beat.

Yeah, why?

Hello, Obsidian! called a chorus of mermaids, all different than those she had met in the square.

Hello, I'm still new, everyone, but respect to your names!

Thank you, Obsidian! answered a red-haired mermaid whose hair was cornrowed down her scalp in various directions.

I'm going to head back; thank you so much for your work!

You are welcome!

Hey, why are we leaving? We didn't even try to feed some of the cuttle-fish yet!

I saw that drum before, Daniel.

What? Where could you have possibly seen some magic underwater drum before?

At my godmother's house!

What! Are you sure it's the same drum? Daniel thought as he paced back and forth along the sand.

Yes. Absolutely, yes, Zelma thought as she hurried back the way they had come to the safety of her private room.

You've got to tell Sorceress Topaz, right?

Yeah. But first, I did tell you that the stone feels alive, didn't I?

Yes, yes, you did.

I think I'm going to ask Tiger Iron.

What?

We're almost back at my room, Zelma added as she turned into the largest building and headed toward the passageway to her chambers.

Okay...

Daniel, you seem less than pleased with my plan to try to connect with the stone.

Isn't this something you need to do with mermaid supervision?

So much of my magic is influenced by what I believe to be true. I do trust my mother more since we talked, but if she's here, inadvertently or not, she'll influence what information I can find if I speak with her first.

I mean, you are probably not wrong, but...

But what?

I'm scared. And if you are going some place in your mind, I won't be able to follow you!

Daniel... Zelma thought reassuringly as she made her way to the pile of large pink bubbles and made herself comfortable on her back.

After your godmother took you the first time, I knew right then I'd do anything to be by your side.

And you are. I promise there is nowhere I can go in my mind that won't lead me back to you. Plus, rationally, I know this stone isn't out to get me. I'm sure of it, Daniel.

Are you saying I should be tired because I've been running across your mind all day?

Basically, Zelma added with a tiny laugh to the bottle she held up above her face.

I love you, Mrs. Cruz. I trust you, too. How do you want to do it?

I was thinking that I could hold on to the stone, close my eyes, and see if she can talk to me. And you'll hang out in the bottle and be prepared to tell anyone who comes to look for me what happened if things get complicated. But I expect that she'll help me see how this stone can be here instead of within my godmother.

Okay. Okay, okay, Daniel thought as he paced the width of the bottle back and forth. *I'm right here.*

Yup. Let's go.

Zelma laid the bottle carefully next to her head, pressed another kiss to it, and then turned her gaze toward the ceiling. She placed her hands on the stone at the center of the moon on her hips. Embarrassed of singing, even in her mind, Zelma chose the middle ground of poetry to reach out to the stone.

Oh, tiger iron stone, respect to your name.

Tell me about your journey, your wants, your fame.

Respect to your name from Obsidian,

Respect to your name from Daniel,

Respect to your name all the same.

That was good on the spot, Zelly.

Thank you, Daniel, Zelma couldn't help but reply in a familiar singsong tone.

You sounded just like Agate!

I couldn't resist. But nothing is happening.

Try repeating it and humming maybe? You went through the work of making it kind of rhyme anyway.

You're right again. I'm going to keep repeating it until I hear something from the other side.

Zelma continued, quietly humming a tune she was creating as she went behind the lyrics in her mind. She started faintly at first before she closed her eyes and thought the song louder.

Oh! It is starting to warm up in my hands! I feel like I can see something.

That's cool because your eyes are still totally closed, Daniel thought back nervously.

Her eyes began to race beneath her lids. The tips of her fingers felt swollen and sensitive as a tiny jolt of what felt like electricity shot out from the stone and buzzed up her arms.

Suddenly, instead of on a bed of unpoppable, pillowy bubbles, she was peering up at the sun on the surface of the water. A ship passed steadily amidst a building storm. Without understanding why, she began to come up with safe ways to topple it as the rain and the wind grew bolder. Some people needed her help and others demanded her vengeance.

With a start, she thought she was waking up in her own life, but looking around, Zelma realized she was in another place entirely. Only this time, she was filthy and chained down in the belly of some wooden beast. The sounds of the ocean and the wind howling were so loud she almost missed the creaking of the wood behind her head being peeled back. She opened her mouth to scream, but her voice was hoarse from the hours she'd screamed already. Once the plank was removed, the water didn't rush in. Instead, she saw a hand with long, golden-brown stiletto nails rush into the boat in the water's place. In the palm of that hand was a familiar black stone. Slowly, she reached to grasp it, and everything went black.

When the light returned, her mind felt different. She closed her eyes to remember where she had been and opened them to find that she was sunning herself on the sands in the dying light of the evening. There were a group of men chasing a woman across the beach. Annoyed with the commotion, she dived into the water up to her waist. She opened her mouth and began to sing. The men, one moment so focused on the woman they were cornering, turned toward the water. They grinned at the sight of a topless woman treading the water, but slowly their eyes grew more and more vacant. They stepped out into the water to find the source of that voice and didn't stop, even when the water covered their heads. Though she was too far away to zero in on the frightened woman's face, Tiger Iron smiled and beckoned the shaking woman closer.

Zelma leaned forward and fell into another dream. She'd landed on her belly, crawling through the muck. She was so caked in putrid, black-brown grime that she couldn't make out what she looked like—only that she was nearly bone thin. The sound of orcas grew louder, echoed by the engine of a boat giving chase. Above her head, the orcas seemed terrified—doing everything to evade capture or death or worse. She licked her lips, and the taste of death that lingered in her mouth made her long to be like them instead of herself, to be one of them and protect them. Maybe she could do it if she just had enough time...

Zelma! There's chanting, singing, and stuff going on outside of the curtain!

D-Daniel?

People are outside the entrance area of your room. I think someone is trying to seal you in.

What?

They took your chain out of your hands. I saw Spinel and maybe Aquamarine, but there were a few more.

Hey! Hey, don't lock me in here! What are you doing? Zelma called out as she sat up.

Stay in here for your own good, Obsidian!

For whose good? Zelma responded but got no reply. *They're gone, huh? I have no idea who that was. How long was I under?*

Long enough for me to be worried, so a few minutes. When the others came, at first I thought they wanted to help you, but—nope! There was nothing I could do but watch, again.

I'm so sorry. But you don't have to worry because we're getting out of here. We are going to warn the others.

Warn them about what?

My godmother wants the stone. I don't really understand what it showed me, but I was her at some point. I was Tiger Iron the day she saved my mother, I'm sure of it.

Uhm, I don't know what to say to that.

It's too much to go into now. She must have a way to use the stone to become sorceress or something.

How can she just become sorceress now?

How or why doesn't matter. What matters now is getting to my mother and letting her know that they're putting their plan in motion. I'm so frustrated with everyone being a step ahead of me down here!

Well, what did you want to try? Every conceivable way out of here is bubbled over.

Zelma rushed toward the beaded curtain and came toward the rounded entrance to her room. The entire archway was filled to the brim with giant, multicolored bubbles. Zelma couldn't shake the thought that the entrance to her room looked like some silly, senior prank. Moving carefully, she poked a bubble, only to watch it nearly swallow her index finger without popping. The bubble held fast to the skin of her finger until she pulled it back far enough to break the connection. *The bubbles, they're so shiny but sticky, too. I'd probably get stuck if I tried to force my way through.*

I bet they thought that's all it would take to keep you in here. How dare they underestimate my wife!

Which is why I should think of something creative, but I literally have no idea where to start...

Breathe with me.

Daniel! We're underwater.

I mean focus with me, okay?

Okay, okay.

What can you think of?

Zelma held his bottle up against the side of her face distractedly as she thought. *I could Call for help.*

Okay, anything else?

The bubbles are made with our magic. Maybe I can use my stone to pop them all? Or clear them?

There you go.

It's so hard to guess about things like this. I thought I knew how the world is supposed to work. Now, all I have are questions. I feel like a kid again in the most annoying way possible, she replied as she leaned back onto the wall next to the doorway and slid down.

I know, but you gotta try, Daniel thought from where his bottle was cradled on her lap.

As she sat on the floor with her head bowed, Zelma realized she was mimicking the statue across the room and stifled a quick laugh. *I'm turning into my mother already.*

Zelma? We can't give up.

You're right. If I hide now, a lot of people will be in danger. I just feel like I get knocked back down every time I get back up, you know?

It's not over until you don't get back up, Zelma.

Yeah, Zelma replied with a small nod. *If this doesn't work, I'll try something else to get out of here.*

Yeah!

Okay. I'll come up with a song to help me focus my energy.

Sure, I'll give you a beat, Daniel thought as he playfully cupped his hands around his mouth and started to beatbox.

You're ridiculous... But, actually, do it.

Seriously?

Yeah, it's kind of helping.

Zelma allowed the simple beat to play out once, twice before she opened her mouth to recite a poem to the looped sound Daniel gave her.

Sharper than a scalpel, darker than the night.

Earth who made obsidian, strengthen my strike.

Strengthen my strike. Strengthen my strike!

As she'd seen Citrine do in the nursery cave, Zelma clapped her fore-arms together with purpose at the last word.

That's not what I expected, Daniel thought as he took a few deep breaths.

My arms! They're completely stone-looking, but I can still feel them, Zelma thought as she took in the sight of her forearms. They were black, so black that the light reflected off them and looked white in the sharp grooves of the obsidian at the edges.

Those look dangerous!

Well, I thought smooth obsidian might not pop them as quickly.

Can you break through the bubbles?

Zelma held stone fists up in front of her face, as if she were entering a boxing ring, as she turned to face the bubble blockade in her way. *I can try.*

Pulling her fist back, she slammed it forward. The first few bubbles popped on contact, but as she struggled to draw her hand back again, she could tell the bubbles were layered out into the hallway.

I'm going to have to punch and Call for help, I guess. If I break through enough bubbles, it will be easier for someone from another side to dig me out.

Sounds like a good idea, Daniel replied as he stood up on the beach to get a better view.

Help! Citrine! Howlite! Anyone! Help me!

Damn it!

A familiar thought reached Zelma through the soapy film of popping bubbles.

Agate? Can you help me get out of here?

Yeah, I can. I shouldn't, but I can.

What do you mean you shouldn't?

The bubbles began to melt away.

You would've been out of that in another fifteen minutes anyway, Agate projected dispassionately with her arms crossed. She seemed so unlike herself that Zelma was nonplussed.

Agate! Please, come with me. We have to warn the others that something isn't right.

Something hasn't been right for a long time, Obsidian.

Wait, don't tell me...

I shouldn't have to spell it out for you.

But why did you send me to her? I had no idea who I even was!

I didn't think she'd put the chain on you like that. I hoped you would see the truth. We failed our ancestor. Because of us, humanity is out of control. The Sorceress of the Moon, as she's calling herself now, is going to redeem us.

Sorceress of what? Genocide? She wants to pull people into the sea!

They're pulling us out of the sea! Agate replied with a raise of her arms. *In the past half a century, more and more of us have had Farewell Ceremonies earlier and earlier. You don't understand and you won't because you were raised as human. But humans are robbing us of our ability to roam, our lifespan, and the quality of the oceans we live in. If it comes down to us or them, I choose us. I can't let you get in the way of that.*

Wait, Zelma responded, holding her fists up in the only defensive pose she'd learned. *We don't have to fight! Why do we have to do this my godmother's way? Do you really want to have her be your new sorceress?*

No one does. But it's not personal like that. It's about the future, Agate responded, eyeing Zelma's stance and keeping her distance.

Of course, it's personal! Please, just think about this. My godmother isn't entirely wrong, but maybe she's not worth the sacrifice. Agreeing with her will take so much from you that there will be nothing left to enjoy the spoils of her new world.

You are just like her, Agate projected with a look of absolute disgust.

Huh?

You both just meddle with people's heads, Agate thought exasperatedly. *I don't know what to do. But I've helped you as much as I'm going to,* Agate responded as she turned to leave.

No. C'mon. Let's find everyone.

You can go, and I'll head the other way. Whatever happens to you happens, she thought before diving along the hallway that led toward the exit.

Okay then, Agate.

Zelma lowered her arms and they transformed back to normal as she tried to make sense of Agate's change of heart.

Wow, Zelma. How did you know to say all that stuff?

It's what I've been thinking about my godmother. I knew I couldn't be the only one. If you take out the mass murder, then she has a point. But you can be right the wrong way. I'm probably naïve, but we can't just let the world flood. Even if her plan partially succeeds, the oceans could literally salt any earth left behind. We need to stop this!

Yeah, Zelma. But what do we do now?

Maybe we'll figure it out if we head back to the kelp garden? I think being in public is the safest I can be for now if not every pod member is involved.

There were decorative scarves swirling in the ocean currents as soon as she made it out of the hallway. The lights strewn along the path toward the kelp garden blurred past Zelma's vision as she swam frantically toward the stage. She stopped short when she arrived—the drum was no longer innocently waiting on stage. It was now the only thing protecting the modesty of a very tall man. He was handsome enough to be memorable fully clothed. There were not even bubbles escaping from his lips—he managed breathing underwater effortlessly.

He stood, experimentally tapping on the set of drums around his waist with sticks matching the set. He also had pads affixed to the back of his head and both elbows and knees. As he drummed, a wave of sound traveled underwater. He occasionally shouted in rhythm with the beats he created. Sparks of light issued up from the pad at the back of his head. There were already some members of the pod who blatantly fawned over him.

All attention was focused on the stage, and Zelma was undetected as she scanned the area for Citrine. She felt a presence come up behind her and she turned in fright, only to find Citrine had been waiting for her.

Citrine?

Obsidian, you out early? We don't start for a few hours. Are you taking a peek? That's Atlas—the most popular performer there is right now.

Citrine, it's bad! I was locked in my room. I don't know who that man is, but he's using drums that I saw in my godmother's home. Something is happening today, and we've got to stop it!

A wave of intensity washed over Citrine from the crown of her head to the tip of her fins. *They did what to you?* Citrine replied as she carefully placed her hands on Zelma's shoulders.

Zelma inched back instinctively but continued. *There were sticky, rainbow bubbles locking me in my room. My godmother is nearby, she must be. Something is going down, but I don't know what.*

Come with me. Now!

Where are we going again?

There's a committee working on the vent, Obsidian. Citrine turned her head back and continued almost dragging Zelma along.

The thermal vent with the lava? But why is that important?

We voted to fortify the crack in the ground because it's steadily been growing. Before the ceremony, a group was chosen to fortify it. The vent is a huge source of power for those who wield earth magic. Whatever is going down is going to happen near that vent. And Agate was on that committee before she was remanded.

Agate is the one who let me go. Maybe she had a change of heart?

Citrine cut her eyes to Zelma in disbelief and pulled Zelma behind the building that held the meeting hall. *She let you go because she knew you'd be there, Obsidian. I knew she was in on this.* The heat from the crack in the earth was almost unbearable so close.

What's happening over there? Zelma asked with her back against the warm stone behind her. She sunk down until her hips were pressed against the mosaic of crushed iridescent stone on the floor.

Citrine, with all the warmth of her namesake stone, placed her hand on Obsidian's shoulder through the thin fabric of the black, fluffy robe.

We have a plan, Obsidian. When it comes to Howlite and I, it's always the same plan. Get Howlite to stealth their way in, and I stop whatever needs to be stopped. It never fails. Sorceress Topaz is already over there. We get Howlite to discreetly let her know. Then, we flush them out and find an opening from there.

Stop them how?

I'm not talking about killing anyone. We're going to ruin whatever they're doing. Hopefully, we outnumber them. It's been like a disease. A few too many of us think that uniting under this woman will get them what they want. Taking over the world is a violent, ugly thing to do without a guarantee we'd come out on top. There might still be time for another choice.

What is that choice, Citrine?

Hell if I know yet.

I feel stupid, but I don't know, either.

You went and found me, which means you're smart enough to not agree with whatever this is. All we can do today is work with what we know.

You're right. Are you okay with this plan, Daniel? Zelma asked, holding up the bottle to peer into her husband's face.

I am as long as you are, he replied with a nod.

But, Citrine, how can we be sure we trust Howlite?

I'd trust them with my life. Plus, if they have Howlite, it's too late for any of us.

Reaching down, Citrine touched a spot on her collarbone that began to light up. She gestured for Zelma to peek through a huge hole in the wall they were leaned up against just behind the gathered mermaids near the molten vent in the earth's crust. Howlite went still from where they could see them posted at the far edge, high above the proceedings. They made a quick excuse, turned, and swam toward where Citrine, Zelma, and Daniel were tucked out of sight at the intersection of two walls. Howlite found them so easily, it was as if they knew where Citrine was all along.

Citrine? What's the emergency?

That woman is going to try it today.

Hmm. I can't say I'm surprised. She hasn't broken her exile yet, but she's been moving on the pod. Who's in with her?

Agate confirmed.

She really betrayed us and for what?

She might have had a change of heart because she let our girl go, Citrine added reluctantly in the face of Zelma's encouraging look.

We'll see when we get this mess cleaned up.

Wait, Citrine, Howlite—do any of you know my godmother's name?

She used to be Tiger Iron, but she was only just leaving when I was turned.

I've been here. I never knew her name from before, but she'd been here decades. She was always... She was always the way she is now. It just seems like more of us are buying into it, Citrine added.

Zelma looked down to Daniel and back up and nodded for them to continue.

Howlite, is Aquamarine in this committee? Zelma asked.

How'd you guess? Spinel is the lead in the gardens, too. Let's try this, Howlite projected back.

In the flash of an eye, every cell in Howlite's body reoriented itself until they were the exact copy of Obsidian—except for a quietly, furious expression that Zelma doubted she had ever made in her entire life.

Why do you look like me?!

Agate let you escape, right?

Yeah, she did.

If Agate hasn't told the others, then we have an advantage. And if they know because it was a part of some plan, then I, unlike you, can fight, and we still have an advantage, Howlite finished with a smirk.

I'm sure my absence is noticed at the gardens. I'll head over to Sorceress Topaz so they think I just had something to ask, Citrine thought as she started to head back the way Howlite came.

Okay. I'll stick with our girl here to confuse anyone. You see if you can get Sorceress Topaz to Call everyone to the vent for some sort of thank-you speech and have them Call for Obsidian.

Let's draw them out and ruin their plans, Citrine replied, her face as serious as Howlite's was mischievous.

I know that's right.

But wait, if they check for me in my room and I'm not there—

It will give those schemers a heart attack or piss them off. Hopefully, they underestimated you as much as possible.

Yeah... Zelma replied distractedly. Howlite had copied her exact likeness—everything but the dramatic robe she threw on on a whim.

Is it weird talking to yourself? Howlite asked with a rare, gentle smile.

I think so? I also don't know what's going to happen.

Yeah, I'm not going to lie to you—it's bad. But at least I know how this pod thinks. I'd do anything to protect you, Sorceress Topaz, and the pod members who believe we can find a better way.

You aren't as concerned for the whole "drowning of humanity" thing my godmother has planned?

That's neither here nor there for me. If that happens, I'll figure it out then. Right now, we stop them before they get any further.

I can't say I don't admire your way of thinking.

Okay, they're Calling and gathering. Stay here. Huddle against this corner. Can you still see around? Howlite asked, gesturing through the rounded hole in the wall they were hiding behind.

Yeah, Howlite. We can see.

Good. I'm walling you in, but you can easily melt it just like you did those obsidian cuffs you had on your lover, yeah? I trust you—come out when you think it's the right time.

Wait, will I get a chance to talk to you again? Zelma projected as she reached for Howlite. She got a quick fist bump in lieu of anything more comforting.

Stopping communication is the first wave of any attack, Obsidian. I don't know if you'll be able to talk to me the whole time, but trust your instincts. Find an opening.

If I get the chance to train with you and Citrine, I am so taking it.

We're the best. See you soon, okay?

Okay.

And with two hands, Zelma watched Howlite as herself seal her into the corner. Howlite's stone was, at first, milky white with an inky black strip weaving its way through it before blurring out to match the iridescent, opaque stone of the building she was leaning against.

You're shaking, Zelma. I'm so sorry I can't help you more.

Me? I'm sorry I am putting you in danger. But I'm going to handle this however I can, Zelma replied as she held Daniel up to see out of the rounded hole they were watching from.

Look, look, look—everyone is coming.

Yeah, they are. There's so many of us, Daniel.

There weren't enough colors in the rainbow for all the shades of scales gathered near the vent. The sorceress was at the center of the large group, floating slightly above to be easily seen. She gestured for someone to part through the crowd.

Look at how awkward Agate is seeing you standing next to Sorceress Topaz.

Zelma's eyes darted around until she focused in on Agate's familiar banded colors near the front of the crowd where she fidgeted in place.

Shhh, let me focus on listening!

Pod members, we are gathered here today to welcome the new person into the pod. My daughter is taking her rightful place, and I couldn't be more hopeful for the future of our pod. Though we still have prepara-tions to make, I wanted to take some time to connect with you all. I won't take too long, for the sake of the cuttlefish in the gardens expecting a buffet. For so many of you to welcome Obsidian and give her advice and care has meant so much to me. It inspires me—

Zelma?

Yeah?

It's a big deal that all of the mermaids give the sorceress respect on her name and talk to her a certain way, right?

Yeah, why?

Some of them aren't listening.

What do you mean?

They're slowly turning their backs to her or looking around for something.

Daniel, you're right!

She's lost control like a substitute teacher on the last day of school.

Suddenly, in a wave of disorienting sound, a black cloud erupted behind the milling crowd of the hundred or so mermaids. Orcas began to pass through the portal and, with a quick turn, rotate back where they came. The wails they made cut communication on and off.

After a moment of anticipation, it wasn't only the orcas breaching the portal. In the midst of the chaos in the enforced silence, Zelma spotted her godmother casually grasping the tale of an orca who slowed to a stop as the others, one by one, no longer came back through.

In a rare moment of vulnerability, the last orca hovered at her godmother's side—despite the depth and the lack of air. With restraint, the larger woman placed her forehead to the orca's as she floated above the large, mournful animal. The watching mermaids shifted uneasily but held off on any confrontation until, with a firm shove, her godmother herded the orca back toward the portal and closed it the very second its tail slipped through.

The atmosphere was thick with tension as she turned to address the mermaids gathered in the courtyard. Flourishing under the scrutiny, the woman formerly known as Tiger Iron smirked and shook her head in utter disgust.

I had a plan, you know. A distraction set up and everything. You couldn't let me have even a few hours, could you? Atlas was going to perform for me as I appeared! Yet another thing you've deprived your charges of. Everything always has to be about you, going on and on with your empty, feel-good platitudes. All while I am trying to stage the next steps for our kind.

I can't call you Tiger Iron, can I? Sorceress Topaz spat hatefully.

No one can call you a sorceress with how you're running our heritage into the ground.

Everywhere the mermaids slowly began to get into defensive stances. Some appeared to be trying to reason with one another. It was impossible for Zelma to tell how many had defected, but there were enough to be troublesome.

Stop this madness now. Already you'll have us harm each other and there are no humans even here! Sorceress Topaz demanded. She summoned a staff in her left hand and took on a defensive position with the staff shielding herself and "Obsidian."

I could kill you, the former mermaid projected with a tilt of her head. She stared down on the sorceress. *I know your name. I know your daughter's name, too. Don't make me do that.*

You just think you know hers. I confess, I did wonder why I never had my magic stripped from me.

I have not stooped so low as to kill our kind yet, but that's up to you, she intoned back with a slow smirk. With a snap of her fingers, the chain that had been on Zelma's hips for so long was now wrapped firmly around her wrist in an instant. Zelma gripped her waist in disbelief.

That's the chain you gave Obsidian! Why even give it to her if you're taking it back?

How else would I get it into the palace so easily and have it waiting for me here?

The other mermaids began to surround their new leader and swim in a circle. At first, there were only a few but gradually more and more. Aquamarine and Spinel approached Sorceress Topaz carefully on either side, as her godmother continued her tirade.

I'm going to take back what was mine, Sorceress Cowardess. The burden of leadership is clearly too heavy for you. It's time for me to step into my destiny as Sorceress of the Moon. It's time for the waters to flood the earth.

What nonsense are you talking about? You'll mix us with humans and have them auction off our power, our tails, to the highest bidder! They're dangerous enough. Say you lose the war you're starting? You have no thought for anything beyond your own ambition. You never have! Sorceress Topaz replied with a roll of her eyes.

Topaz! Enough—she's right and you know it! Aquamarine called from the left as Spinel lunged and wrapped her arms around Obsidian with one hand around her throat.

Aquamarine, you forget yourself! Spinel!

Don't make me wound her, Topaz. We can't let this opportunity go. These humans aren't going to stop until everything is destroyed. Please, see reason!

Let go of Obsidian!

You know I'm faster than you, Topaz. She'll heal once we're done and we have a new sorceress. Obey or else, Topaz! Respect to the name of the Sorceress of the Moon!

Yeah, like that power-hungry woman over there is going to make all of your little problems go away.

Obsidian?

In the blink of an eye, Howlite applied pressure to the elbow around their throat and used the second Spinel reacted in shock to free themself and turn to face their would-be captor.

How dare you doom us all to subservience under someone like that, you damn ruby knockoff. Aren't you embarrassed to be licking her tail fins?

Spinel's face soured. *I should've known you were up to something, Howlite.*

The Sorceress of the Moon, feeling the precariousness of the moment, threw up her arms and called out, *Spinel, Aquamarine, gather the others! Lend me your voices. It is time to bring about the dawning of a new era. The tides will turn against humanity. I am no longer Tiger Iron. I am the Sorceress of the Moon!*

Quickly, in practiced motions, the mutinous mermaids swam toward her and began to circle her as they hummed, louder and louder. The mermaids who hadn't defected began to pull the others away, placing their hands over their mouths, doing anything to stop the sound, the movements that were key to the ritual.

With an expression of intense focus, Sorceress Topaz charged with her baton and was held at bay by the bodies of her charges as they swam around the aspiring Sorceress of the Moon.

Tiger Iron, source of all,

Heed my voice,

Respond to my Call.

Tiger Iron, by spirit I believe,

That by your power,

An era I will conceive.

Tiger Iron, your destruction be a sign,

Strip back the years and give me what's mine

Reward me with a moment in time.

153

Reward me with a moment in time.

What is she doing?

Don't you see the lava rising, Daniel? The vent is becoming unstable! Zelma replied as she watched the earth begin to shift and the thermal vent widen.

We need to help them!

Daniel, she's trying to go back.

Back where?

She wants to destroy the stone to harness its power for some way to change the past. That's got to be it!

Wait, so that means if she succeeds, she might make it so your parents don't meet?

Maybe? I might not be born possibly, unless they meet some other way. There's no idea what could happen.

I don't want to live in a world you weren't born into.

The same for you. I don't think you'd survive the world being flooded, either. Our families are in danger, everything is.

By tacit agreement, they turned their eyes toward the unfolding conflict. Citrine cleared a path wherever she moved—with strategically thrown elbows and swipes of her tail, she was effectively disrupting the chanting wherever she got close enough. Although they tried, there weren't enough mermaids to defend against the bulk of Citrine's efforts.

You heard what Howlite said. I need to find my moment.

Okay, we find our moment.

Do you want me to leave you here? For someone to find in case... In case I don't make it?

No! I'll honor my vows. I can't protect you the way I want to, but I can be near you. You're my wife and I couldn't live, not even somewhere as nice as this vacation in a bottle, with the thought that I let you abandon me.

Okay! We'll cry later. You see that portal opening up above my godmother?

Yeah, I can see it, Daniel replied, turning his attention to the growing purple ball of cloudy energy swirling with the circular movements of the mermaids humming and singing along with her.

I think she's going to put the chain in there because how else would you put something in lava without getting burned? I think she's going to use the vent to destroy the stone and somehow use the magic to go back in time.

But doesn't the stone have, like, a soul? You said it was alive.

She is alive. I don't know how my godmother could do this. The stone shared memories with me. I barely got a chance to tell you everything I'd seen. It makes sense why my godmother is so reckless, though.

What do you mean?

She probably thinks none of this matters. Like a video game or something.

Why couldn't she just ask the stone to take her back in time or whatever?

I have no idea if that's how any of this works. But if I get the stone away from her like all the other pod members are fighting to do, then that's got to be the first step, right?

Right.

We aren't even that far. I don't know how no one has noticed me.

There's a lot going on...

This is probably rash, but I think I have a plan. If I watch Howlite and Citrine, maybe I can use a path they clear in the fighting to get to that portal...

The portal above her head? The portal that leads to the lava?

Yeah. Daniel... In case this is it, just know that I—

It's not over. Tell me after, alright?

O-okay. I'm sure there will be time.

Focusing her magic, Zelma felt the edges of her fingers and the tip of her nose harden into her namesake. She watched back and forth as flashes of scales in every conceivable color swam laps around the courtyard.

Citrine, Zelma Called with all her focus, *I need a path to my godmother.*

Citrine turned her head toward where Zelma and her husband were concealed and nodded. Zelma quickly melted the stone Howlite had set in place. With a burst of focus, she summoned her shield and hardened her fists. She came quickly around the corner and charged toward the cheery, fiery bright shine of Citrine's scales. Together they made a beeline for the so-called Sorceress of the Moon.

Swimming in the after currents of Citrine gave Zelma incredible speed. Any manicured hand that grabbed for her was foisted away by Citrine ahead of her, and those who tried to chase her were seconds behind.

For a moment, everything slowed down. She saw the look of rage and confusion on her mother's face as she blocked a blast of magic with a spin of her staff. She looked into her godmother's fully black, empty eyes and saw the dawning comprehension as Zelma pulled a hand off her shield. Zelma clasped her hand around her godmother's wrist and, with one deft movement, uncoiled the chain.

You! You and your useless mother always think you can interfere with my plans. You are too late. You can melt along with the stone for all I care. If you're in the next life, I'll train you better, Obsidian.

Obsidian! No! Zelma grasped that there was more than one person projecting the thought, but before she could respond, her godmother grabbed her around the waist and threw her into the portal above her head like a ragdoll.

In a sick parody of her transformation, she felt the urge to give in to the heat attacking her bones. Thinking quickly, she attempted to call on her magic to harden herself into stone fully. With a scream, she managed it but knew she was stalling the inevitable. The lava was closing in around her and the stone in her hand was already being consumed.

Daniel! Can you hear me?

I love you, Zelma! Daniel replied from where he was backed up against a tree on the farthest end of the beach.

I love you, too!

She turned to go back through the portal, but there was nothing there. She shielded Daniel's bottle and with all her might Called for help one last time.

Help me! Is anyone there?

Obsidian.

Through the haze and heat of being inches away from being consumed by lava, Zelma struggled to see—but her mind, not her eyes, supplied the vision. She saw a woman with her afro like a soft cloud above her head. There were jewels strewn through her hair, every type imaginable. She was cloaked in layered scarves of brown and blue and maroon, and the scales on her tail were a banded blend of the same.

Obsidian, I am being released. The ritual is almost complete.

No... I tried so hard...

I know. That's why I'm giving my power to you, Obsidian.

Tiger Iron? Zelma questioned the figure before her. In a blink, the woman who floated in the lava above her changed. There were no bangles, no claws, no scales. Just sporadically scarred, occasionally stretch-marked, ordinary deep-brown skin. Her face was alight with the everyday Zelma recognized from her aunts, her cousins, her friends. And yet her eyes were wise—she seemed both in her thirties and a hundred years old simultaneously.

My power is fading. The former Tiger Iron no longer bears one of my stones. She's now a stranger to me. Just like the first Obsidian I saved all those years ago—take my offering. I will always, always find you.

Tiger Iron held out her palm. Zelma saw the same rounded chunk of obsidian from her memory, and she reached for it.

There's no time. Think of a moment! The last moment you were safe. Hurry! cried Tiger Iron.

Daniel!

Zelma!

There was a blinding light, but it was cooling. Just as quickly as her mind could process that sensation, she was standing again on her own two feet.

"You may now kiss the bride."

Daniel, life-sized once more, cradled her face in his shaking hands. She leaned in even before he could, and their tears mingled as they kissed first once, then over and over as they gently bit at each other's lips and sighed. It wasn't until the hoots and cheers from their audience that they realized anyone else was there at all.

With resolve, they looked into one another's eyes.

"Happily ever after is just the beginning," Zelma sighed. Neither of them could stifle their laughter.